THE CHAINBREAKERS

THE CHAINBREAKERS

Julian Randall

Henry Holt and Company
New York

Henry Holt and Company, *Publishers since 1866*
Henry Holt® is a registered trademark of Macmillan Publishing Group, LLC
120 Broadway, New York, NY 10271 • mackids.com

Our books may be purchased in bulk for promotional, educational, or
business use. Please contact your local bookseller or the Macmillan Corporate
and Premium Sales Department at (800) 221-7945 ext. 5442 or by email at
MacmillanSpecialMarkets@macmillan.com.

Library of Congress Cataloging-in-Publication Data

Names: Randall, Julian, author.
Title: The chainbreakers / Julian Randall.
Description: First edition. | New York : Henry Holt and Company, 2024. |
  Audience: Ages 8–12. | Audience: Grades 4–6. | Summary: Thirteen-
  year-old Violet Moon takes on the role of Reaper captain after her
  father is captured by the sinister Children of the Shark, forcing her to
  navigate perilous waters to rescue him and save the world from the
  ghost-shark threat.
Identifiers: LCCN 2023045216 | ISBN 9781250882028 (hardcover)
Subjects: CYAC: Fantasy. | Fathers and daughters—Fiction. | Rescues—
  Fiction. | Sharks—Fiction. | Ghosts—Fiction. | LCGFT: Fantasy fiction. |
  Novels.
Classification: LCC PZ7.1.R36665 Ch 2024 | DDC [Fic]—dc23
LC record available at https://lccn.loc.gov/2023045216

First edition, 2024
Book design by Aurora Parlagreco
Printed in the United States of America by Lakeside Book Company,
Harrisonburg, Virginia

ISBN 978-1-250-88202-8
10 9 8 7 6 5 4 3 2 1

For my people, who come from survivors and song

The boat we was on had physics
That left some of us swimmin'

—Saba, "Few Good Things"

— PROLOGUE —

Once, there were men who sought to chain the world—and so, they began with our ancestors, the Sun People.

We were children of a gold continent, a place where the sun hung in the sky and the people stretched their Black, Black hands to drink in the warmth. The people, our people, danced and held one another, thought and remembered and created and ran. They wrote great stories of the world they knew, and they formed cities, and everywhere the sun found the people, the sun found love.

The men who sought to chain the world, the Chainmakers, wanted people they could hold as animals and break until they were tools, building their cities, speaking their tongue, and hauling their crops to feed their children. And so, the men who sought to chain the world constructed rotten ships to steal the Sun People and their Black, Black hands, to steal their songs from the winds of their homeland. The ships spread like a plague, and the men who used their hands to bind the hands of others grew sicker and crueler with each breath.

The Sun People fought where they could, but the Chainmakers were too many. They hauled the strongest of the Sun People into ships to drag them across the ocean. Though the Sun People prayed to the gods they knew for anything that might free them from this tragedy, their prayers went unanswered for a time, and many died of disease or starved, too thin to make a noise.

The gods of the old world and the new seemed to weep, for they did not know how to undo what the world was becoming.

But the gods are always listening, even the ones we don't yet know we are praying to.

The gods of the old world and the new, gods beneath the tides and above, looked to the ocean and saw that the Sun People's prayers had turned to rebellion. And the gods knew rebellion was a storm they could deliver.

The Storm at the Edge of the World raged for days without the skies knowing peace. Some of the Sun People saw that it was finally their chance to strike. They shattered their chains and stole control of the ships from the Chainmakers, and they thanked the eye of the storm for their lives. The Sun People became their own Chainbreakers. And then, the ocean that had swallowed so many of the Sun People opened for the ships of the Chainbreakers, and their ships descended beneath the waves and found refuge.

The ocean parted, and the five leaders of the rebellion sailed their ships down and down into a world where there was water above and water below but air in between—the Tides of the Lost—where we now live. On the water, the Sun People found so many of their lost kin and pulled their souls—souls of their siblings and elders of the continent—into their ships as if they were reaping a great crop.

And the gods of the old world and the new were impressed by how the Chainbreakers cared for the dead as Passengers and siblings. So the gods offered these first Reapers a gift.

And the gods cursed the Chainmakers.

The Chainbreakers were called Reapers by the gods of the old world and the new and decided to make their Five Heavens on the Tides of the Lost.

And so, the Reaper ships spread to every corner of the map, and each found an island to call their Heaven. The first ship, fast as a moony, set out to see how far south the ocean ran, and these became the first Reapers of the Heaven of Horizon. The boldest warriors among the Reapers admired how their ship had cleaved through the storm clouds like a blade, and they sailed north to what would become the Heaven of Shard, sharpening their spears and tongues to any enemy. The growers and farmers found themselves pulled to the sweet scent of the harvest lands beneath a baobab tree that scraped the bottom of the sky and drank the light of the stars, and so those Reapers grew to call their Heaven Root. Nearby, a fourth ship set off to build a great city for every Passenger reaped from the waters; so many reached out their hands to the living and the dead that they named their home Palm. And finally, the curious, the scientists, the inventors, and the dreamers pulled their ship to where the tops of waves chopped fierce as teeth, and thus named their Heaven Crest.

And for a brief time, all was well on the Tides of the Lost . . . until the Chainmakers returned, mutilated by the hunger of an unbroken curse. They became the Children of the Shark, souls bound to hunt Passengers who hit the water. They became the Depths they dragged the souls down to. They became the teeth beneath the tide.

For a moment, as the demons erupted from the water, the Reapers did not know how they could fight ghosts of cruel men with the heads of sharks. But the Reapers had magic of their own, pieces of the storm they could command.

Some of the Reapers told stories of great warriors from their village, stories of tricksters and knives that danced in the air. The wind, hearing such stories, threaded itself together to form weapons of air and joined the Reapers in battle. Other Reapers watched the tides and navigated to wherever there were Passengers to snatch from the jaws of these shark-demons. And still other Reapers became Stormcallers who spilled their rage into the sky until the air was choked with heavy clouds and thunder reigned over the tides.

Together, the Reapers cheered and laughed as the enemy

retreated. They looked above them and spread their Black, Black hands beneath the moon of their new home and said, "This is our Heaven now, we the Reapers of the Five Heavens, the tides where no one is lost forever. This will be our home, no matter what trouble dims the stars."

— 1 —

Lately the stars are dim, but that's never stopped us before. The purple hours stretch across the sky just like they did the hour my mother named me Violet. The ship, our ship, the *Moony*, sways and bucks just like it has all twelve years of my life. The sprawl of the navy sail ripples quietly as the Windthreaders stir the breeze.

But still, there's a weight in my stomach. I can't put my finger on it as I sweep a braid away from my face, staring hard at the tides.

"Why does today feel so different?" I mumble to myself, the waves rising and crashing with my thoughts.

"Well, maybe," says a deep, gravelly voice as I feel a hand on my shoulder.

I don't let the voice finish. My fingers slip instantly to the small steel blade at my hip as I wheel around, tossing it into the air in a flashy arc and catching it in my opposite hand.

"Whoa there, Little Fish." My father's silver smile flashes

like the blade. "It's just me! Please don't let *this* be the mutiny that finally takes me out."

I relax and feel the blood rush to my cheeks, scowling at his teasing grin. "You shouldn't sneak up on people."

"It's my ship; I can definitely afford to do some sneaking!" Dad shrugs. "Now, are you planning on sheathing that? Or is this gonna be a *very* different father-daughter conversation than I thought?"

I bite my lip and sheath my knife. "Don't you have steering to do, Old Man?"

I stare up at the sky, looking for the signal flare from Mooneye and Sunshower at the stern.

Dad claps his hand to his chest in a mock wound. I roll my eyes. The crew lets him play too much; he already has command of the *Moony*, so I don't see why we all must suffer through his comedy, too.

"Always in such a rush. There will be plenty of Passengers to save when you're captain." Dad squeezes a calloused brown hand on my shoulder. The Mark of the Scythe—the dim blue tattoo indicating his status as the ship's captain—gleams on his mahogany forearm. "Speaking of Passengers, can you go find Moss? We need to start getting the newly rescued souls below deck so the Pointers don't—"

He stops when he sees my mouth twitch down at the corners. He doesn't need to explain to me why we must get the souls below deck quickly. We Reapers of the Five Heavens aren't the only force on the Tides of the Lost. Our sworn enemies, the

Children of the Shark, are what became of the Chainmakers when they fell from their ships during the Storm at the Edge of the World. The fanged ghost-shark hybrids, who we call Pointers for short, are drawn to the souls of Passengers.

Dad notices my silence and frowns as he stares at my sword belt. "Your mother would have been so proud."

I try to laugh it off, but my voice sounds a little hollow. Today must be even stranger than I thought: Dad *never* brings up Mom unprompted. Not since the day she was killed fighting what Dad says was the biggest Pointer he'd ever seen. Pointers don't drag Reapers down into the water like they do with Passengers. But if they stab you, you're gone, forever. And you never become a Passenger.

Ever since Mom died when I was seven, on their last mission together, I've been at Dad's side as his honorary first mate.

Sometimes the Children of the Shark attack ships, but mostly they try to capture souls the moment they reach the Tides of the Lost, before we Reapers can transport them to safety in the Five Heavens. It wasn't too long ago, on my first mission, that I saved Moss from a pack of Pointers when he first crashed down into the water. I still remember the sickly gray-green light bubbling up from below.

Actually, that's a really good question. Where is that little trick-of-the-light anyway?

I want to tell Dad I can handle more responsibility. I can fight better than most of the crew, and I can navigate, and I can tie any knot faster than everyone but Gourd, his actual first mate. Plus, the first three times Dad transferred the Mark of the Scythe to me—so I could feel the flow of the magic that holds the ship together—we only almost crashed *once*. That's, like, 2:1 odds, maybe better, that I'll be the greatest Reaper captain the tides have ever known! Just because I'm a kid on a ship doesn't mean the only other kid on the ship is *all* I can handle.

But all that has to wait.

The sky splits with lightning as the tides churn beneath us. Three balls of pulsing blue light zip out ahead of the ship as Sunshower's arrows signal to the crew that we've arrived to answer the call. Every Reaper ship has a Tidewatcher that helps the ship navigate to Passengers before the Children of the Shark can snatch them down to their lair in the Depths. Reapers have petty rivalries among ourselves, including differences of opinion in what it even means to *be* a Reaper, but at the end of the day, we all want to get the Passengers to safety. We just have different approaches to how we use our magic to do it. Sometimes we get in each other's way, and that's how Passengers can get lost in seconds.

As if the tides could hear my thoughts, I squint at the horizon and see the outline of the Shard Reapers' ship, the *Stormblade*, which is at least twice the size of the *Moony*. The Reapers of Shard dye their hair white as starlight to honor the Passengers. And they are extremely powerful Stormcallers, but sometimes it can really make things difficult for everyone else on the waters when they—

Thunder booms, and I roll my eyes as a towering wave of water crashes over the bow of our ship.

"YOU'D THINK THOSE DYE-HEADS WOULD LEARN TO AIM THEIR MAGIC, BUT NOOOO."

No Reaper ship is a bigger pain in the neck to deal with on a mission than the *Stormblade*.

"VIOLET!" Dad calls, his eyes glowing a faint cobalt blue that matches the glowing Mark of the Scythe on his forearm. "Get to the Ropers, now!"

I'm already spinning on my heel to go secure my rope with the other Ropers. Dad maneuvers the *Moony* closer to where I can see a huddle of Passengers struggling to stay afloat in the water, crying out, confused, and far from the reach of the Reapers of the *Stormblade*. I want to swing in and rescue them, but then I see a familiar sickly gray-green glow spread below the water near us. A foul smell bubbles up around us like a smile stuffed with rotten teeth. All the sound rushes out of my ears as I watch a hook shoot up from the water, landing heavily and punching into the deck of our ship. The chain behind it pulls taut with a rusted scream.

Just like that, we are being boarded by the Children of the Shark.

2

The rusted chain screeches while the glowing hook sinks deeper into the wood like a fang.

Wonderful. Time for the fun part.

"NOT ON MY SHIP!" I holler, kicking the hook with all my might. The hook wiggles, but it's embedded into the wood, so it won't come loose—and plunge the enemy overboard before they can attack. The Children of the Shark start climbing along the edge of the ship. Dad's eyes are surging with blue energy as all his concentration guides the ship over the greedy waves.

"Not. Today." I kick again and the grappling hook loosens even more, but it's still lodged in the wood. Chains clink louder now behind me from port as first one ghostly hand, then another, hauls itself onto the *Moony*. The Pointers have come to try to steal any Passengers they can get their claws on.

"I said"—I wind up for one last kick—"not today!"

I slam my boot into the side of the hook, shielding my

eyes from flying splinters, and it finally comes free. It plummets into the water, carrying the boarding party with it. Thunder cracks above us again from Stormcaller magic, an enormous boom that echoes in the clouds.

"Leave it to Shard to steal my moment." I sigh, wheeling around to see six more chains find purchase on the opposite side of the ship, some with Pointers already boarding.

"I keep forgetting"—I roll my eyes, drawing my knife— "you guys really like to dance!"

The Children of the Shark snarl at my joke. They stare at me, eyes dull and filmy, noses to the air, hunting for Passengers. I wrinkle my nose at the scent of foul seawater dripping onto the deck. One Pointer strips seaweed from its torso, while others fidget with the smoky gray rags they drape over their chiseled pearl-white bodies. I stare at them for a moment, watching their beady eyes and finned forearms, their faces like men with the teeth and hammerheads of sharks.

As the tallest Pointer roars and lightning cleaves the sky, instead of immediately seeking Passengers to steal like they usually do, the Pointers charge right at Dad, who stands frozen in place, jaw set in determination as he channels all his energy to steer the *Moony* to safety.

What the?!

Pointers never go for Reapers first. They fight Reapers that get in the way of them stealing Passengers. They board our ships to distract, to intercept Passengers who we just pulled out of the water, the Passengers already waiting in the belly of the ship. But even then, they always go straight below deck to try and steal Passengers while the crew is occupied.

Are they evolving? Is this all a trap? It's an ambush. Leave it to the Pointers to fight dirty, to stab my dad with his back turned just like they did my mother. I have to reach him. My heartbeat thuds in my ears as I feel myself running toward them.

My brain is spinning like a compass needle trying to piece together a spell, any magic, to protect my dad.

I don't know much magic of my own yet. Most Reaper captains can do a bit of every type: Tidewatching, Wind-threading, Stormcalling. We generally learn once the command of the ship is being transitioned. So there's only so much I've been able to pick up from the books I've borrowed without permission. *But* luckily, Gourd, Dad's first mate, did *finally* teach me one spell from the Windthreaders. And I know those drooling Pointers are going to absolutely hate it, which is just a bonus.

"Silent friend, who watches all stories, song beneath songs," I recite between huffs. I feel the air warm around my palms, the magic calling the wind to me, and the wind agreeing to follow. *"Gather to me, old friend, raucous friend. Gift me with your Thousand Knives!"*

The breeze surges around my arms with magic. I grin sharply. It must have worked! With Windthreader magic, it's not enough to know the words; you have to convince the wind to mimic what you're saying. The warm air croons its approval of my story and curls around the knife in my hand. The air around me swirls, forming many copies of my knife above my head, poised to strike at my command.

The first pair of Pointers has almost reached Dad, who's still frozen with the strain of trying not to let the Shard Reapers' storm smash the ship to matchsticks. Oily black saliva drips from row upon row of translucent fangs in the Pointers' mouths, each of them aimed at his neck.

Not today.

I flick my wrist and watch the first wind-knife bury itself in one of the creatures' shoulders. I slide across the slick deck and drive a kick into the side of the second Pointer's knee. It lets out a wet scream as the leg buckles. I see the Pointer's beady eyes go wide as another one of the wind-blades finds its mark. It squeals and collapses forward, and I barely roll away to avoid it falling on me. It's probably half my weight, but I keep a strong policy of not letting shark-demons touch me.

Especially when they brought friends. And the Children of the Shark? They always bring lots of friends.

I straighten from my roll to see more of the Pointers closing the distance between me and Dad. The rest of the crew must be on rope duty, helping pull the new Passengers we came to rescue from the water.

The next wave of eight Pointers has fanned out. More are boarding the ship, attacking from multiple directions as the crew rushes out to fight and stop them. I tighten my grip on my knife. As a leaping Pointer crashes down next to me, I swing up just in time to deflect the serrated fin on its forearm. This one was quick, swinging his other arm at my head. Though I dodged most of the blow, I feel hot blood dripping along my cheek from a fresh cut. I stumble back, then explode forward, tackling the creature to the ground as it thrashes beneath me. I bring the blade down into its chest and roll off just before the ghost-shark dissipates into the air as it dies.

I spring up, ready to go another round with the remaining Pointers trying to make a run at Dad. He's slowing the ship, eyes on the water as the *Moony* pulls level with some Passengers desperately swimming away from the spreading glow of the Children of the Shark. If we can't take out these Pointers soon, who knows what might happen to both Dad and the Passengers.

As if the universe heard my thoughts, a second later a woman lands beside me, kneeling on the deck. The patterns shaved into her tight fade gleam in the half-light. Gourd's already barking orders to nearby crew members before she even finds her footing.

"Violet! Ropers! Now!" Gourd bellows, driving a knee into the jaw of a Pointer.

"But what about—" I start rushing toward Dad but feel a gust of wind push me away from the fight.

I know it's not worth arguing. Dad always says, *Mind the*

Passengers, not the storm. I just wish he didn't have to mean it so literally.

The rain is slick beneath my boots as I duck and spin around more crew members now locked in combat with the boarding Pointers. By the time I reach Moss, I find him holding the last of the thick ropes anchored to the ship in his branch-thin arms, a determined look on his face.

"Moss, what in the Five Heavens are you doing above deck? What happened to the rest of the Ropers—" The question dies in my throat as I see that the Ropers' ropes are severed. Must've been the Pointers. I sprint to the edge of the railing, eyes scanning the waters, but there's no sign of Ropers or Passengers or the dead in the churning waves. Only the Children of the Shark's ethereal glow is visible. In the chaos of the storm and the boarding, we hadn't seen them pull our Passengers into the Depths.

"WHERE DID THEY TAKE THEM, MOSS?! DID YOU SEE?" My voice competes with the bellow of thunder.

But I know before he even opens his mouth to respond that it's too late. By now, those Passengers are most definitely being dragged down into the Depths, where we'll never see them again.

Moss is standing near the railing, about to answer, when I hear the ocean roar as a huge wave rolls beneath the ship. I feel my heart skip a beat as Moss reaches for my hand, misses, and topples over the ship's side. He hovers, just for a second, floating above the tides, drifting down slowly in the violent wind. I don't even hear a splash.

"MOSS!" I scream, my voice raking my throat raw.

I'm about to leap into the waters when I wheel around and see Dad barreling toward me. All in one fluid motion, I feel him tug the rope from me with one hand and clasp my forearm with something hot as he flashes an exhausted grin.

"Hang on to this for me, will you, Little Fish?"

And with that he dives into the waiting tides like an arrow shot straight down into the water.

Lightning screams across the sky, flashing until everything is stop-motion. Dad pulls Moss to him. Darkness, then more darkness. Then more lightning as Dad whispers another story to the winds, and I watch the rope start to levitate Moss back up toward the ship.

Just in time for that sick green light to bubble below them. Just in time for a thickly muscled Pointer to leap up from the tides and grab Dad by the legs. Then another is glomming on, everything anchoring Dad down, down, down.

No! Pointers only take Passengers! Dad's not a Passenger.

I am frozen, my forearm burning.

No, this is a bad vision, a nightmare.

I find my voice and cast up the wind-blade spell. I command them toward the water, and each magic blade sinks into the back of a Pointer. My nightmares always end when I start to fight back. This shouldn't be any different.

I can make this not real.

But it's real. It's all real.

Real as the twenty more Pointers, who bubble up from the water, weighing down Dad. Real as the sickly light of the Children of the Shark as they pull Dad down, down, down into the Depths until the rope snaps and he disappears beneath the restless water.

It's all real.

Real as the heat on my forearm where Dad cupped it before he disappeared beneath the waves. I look and find the Mark of the Scythe, a shimmering lavender tattoo, seared into my skin.

Lightning dims over the water. All the sound bleeds out of the world around me. I blink rain from my eyes, staring at the Mark of the Scythe transitioned to . . . me?

"I'm the . . . I'm the captain now?" I finally say just as two heavy thuds sound off behind me.

I realize Moss has been tugging at my sleeve, apologizing, then looking back out to the water where my father disappeared below the waves. I shove him behind me and wheel to face the new arrivals, ready to knock some Pointers out, but instead I see Gourd and Sunshower mouthing at me. I shake my head and the sound rushes back, the sound of thunder draining away as the *Stormblade* hightails into the distance.

"For the third time—" Gourd starts shouting before Sunshower places a hand to her shoulder, and she calms slightly.

"Violet, where is your father?" Sunshower steps in, his normally laughing eyes narrowed and scanning the deck.

Gourd interrupts, "The *Stormblade* is leaving. All Passengers are aboard, and if we don't turn the ship around quickly, we'll be overrun by Pointers in moments. But I need to get word to Virgil . . ."

All the color drains from Gourd's face as first she, then Sunshower, see the pulsing purple tattoo on my forearm.

"No, there's no way. He'd never be that irresponsible," Gourd says in a voice louder than she realizes.

"VI, LOOK OUT!" Moss pulls me down.

I shove Moss away, hot with anger at the interruption, until I see that a hammerhead Pointer is clinging one armed to the side of the ship nearest me. It hauls itself over the side, making its way toward me, eyes fogged over and fangs out.

"Violet, don't move, I'm coming!" Sunshower pulls his bow from his side and looses two shots that find their marks in the Pointer's shoulder. It pauses and screams, the smell of its waterlogged breath like a poisonous cloud. Then it snaps the arrows, leaving the points buried in its shoulder and retrains its gaze on me. Gourd is preparing her own spell to the wind, but there's no time because the Pointer is already right above me.

And none of it makes sense—Pointers don't take humans. They kill and fight humans, but never capture, never kidnap. We're supposed to protect Passengers, and now I'm the captain and I couldn't even protect my dad from being the only human the Children of the Shark ever stole.

I just need a second to think, to reach my knife, to get to my feet. I just need . . .

"ENOUGH!" I cry and feel the winds rush to my aid, no spell required with the Mark on my forearm. The blast of wind slams into the Pointer, carrying its pearly ghost body out over the tides so fast it skips like a stone launched from a sling.

"Tides, be patient." Gourd rushes over and pulls me to her chest before holding me at arm's length. "Even in death, Virgil really is never out of surprises."

I want to tell Gourd that Dad isn't dead, that I saw him taken. I know he wouldn't die without saying goodbye, even if I can't prove it.

But I don't say anything because her hand is like a vise on my tattooed arm. A warm power like honey floods my veins. The tattoo pulses brighter, and I know without looking at Gourd's face, or Moss's face, or seeing the bright laugh lines of Sunshower's face go straight as an arrow, that we are all thinking the same thing. I am the captain now.

Two pulses of blue sparks rise from the back of the ship as Gourd asks, "Did Virgil teach you how to transfer the Mark back?"

"No." My voice sounds flat, far away, as the magic spreads to my shoulder blades and I feel myself stand a little taller. No wonder Reaper captains always have such good posture. Me? I usually slump like a sad wave.

"He said to hold on to it for him."

"Okay, but the thing is," Sunshower begins as he nocks an arrow to his bow and fires at another boarding Pointer, "we need to get out of here."

He draws another arrow, and the point severs the rope, resulting in a satisfying splash.

"And I don't mean to be pushy but . . . maybe, like . . . now?"

Gourd's eyes narrow.

"Violet, this is not the time for childish games."

"Then it's a good thing no one is playing," I shoot back before I can think of what else to say.

"Excuse me?" Gourd cocks an eyebrow.

"Okay, um, friends." Sunshower's voice slides in between us. "In a perfect world, I have infinite arrows and infinite patience and an infinite stream of smoked fish for which I never have to pay." Another twang of the bow, another hit. "But in reality, I only have infinite skill and eight arrows. So maybe we ought to settle this back at Horizon?"

"I agree!" Moss pipes up.

Gourd rolls her eyes, but she releases my arm. "Fine, we settle it back at Horizon." Gourd pulls off one glove, then another, and reaches out her hands toward me. "Violet, I pray to the gods of the old world and the new that Virgil taught you how to steer."

4

"In some ways, yes?" I say, hating how it sounds like a question.

Dad did teach me how to steer the ship; I've just never done it after my only remaining family had been hauled overboard. Gourd's brow slightly creases before she puts her hands back out again and stares at them until I take them. I feel the powers of the Mark of the Scythe making their way under my skin and surging within me as her magic helps me awaken mine. The warm, magical feeling cycles from my hands to hers, and the power curls up within us until I can barely feel the rain or hear the twang of Sunshower's bow.

"Piloting a ship, like anything else, requires a quiet mind," Gourd says in a deep voice that echoes in my head. "Even during the Storm at the Edge of the World, the first Reapers found their home on the tides by being listeners, allowing the music in the tides to pull them home."

I feel my power respond in prickles, like my hand has fallen asleep.

"Close your eyes, strip away all noise, trust that the dark is a friend, and you will not sink in it."

"Wouldn't it help for her eyes to be open?" Moss asks, tapping his little chin. "Because she is steering?"

"It would help if she trusted the expert and wasn't interrupted," Gourd replies flatly.

I want to tell Gourd not to talk to Moss that way, but Sunshower has started counting his remaining arrows, each shot finding its mark in a shark-demon's heart.

"And that's five . . . Truly we can start moving at any time!"

Gourd squeezes my hands, and gives a 'trust me' nod.

"Four . . . No, wait . . . Three. Oh sorry, false alarm. It's still four but . . ."

I let the dark swallow my vision, listening for the tides. They sound different, a kind of long, high note hidden just under the crash of each wave. Steering with Dad never felt like this, like I *was* the ship and not just on it. Like we were one, and I could feel every speck of sea salt and the shimmer of the moon glowing down along the bow of the ship, hear the dim conversation of the Passengers below, guarded by the rest of the crew. In that moment, I know that I am their captain and responsible for their safety. We need to get home.

Home.

Thinking of it makes all the music beneath the waves sing more clearly. When I open my eyes, the ship begins to yawn into a turn. Toward Horizon, toward home. I am doing it. Even Gourd smiles as the *Moony* picks up speed, the Windthreaders near the mast wasting no time, urging the wind into the mainsail until we are racing toward the Heaven of Horizon. The magic that holds the ship together purrs in my blood, and for a second I can almost forget why and how I just became probably the youngest Reaper captain in history.

"You're doing it, Vi!" Moss cheers, punching the air as Sunshower slings his bow back over his shoulder.

"Nicely done, Captain." He smiles warmly, the dyed tips of his locks dancing before his face with proud laughter. "I'm at your command."

Sunshower salutes and Gourd follows suit, a grimace crossing her face.

"Indeed, Captain." Gourd swallows hard, as if the words taste bitter. "You did well, all things considered. And now you will always be able to find that space of calm again. No matter how many lights go out."

My question is a hard stone in my throat, but I push it out anyway. "What do we do now?"

Sunshower squints uncomfortably, scratching the back of his head. "The thing is, somebody really ought to make 'The Speech' sooner than later? Just so the Passengers aren't, um . . ."

"Confused? Scared? Worried they went with the wrong ship?"

"Yes, Moss," Sunshower cuts in. "Any of those reasons would be very helpful."

"The girl just lost her father," Gourd snaps at Sunshower. "I will give the speech."

"The captain gives the speech," I say quietly, feeling the ship slow a touch as my concentration drifts more toward the conversation.

"Yes, traditionally they do, but . . ." Gourd leans toward me. "I just worry that seeing a child at the helm will be more than many can handle."

"That child"—I feel my mouth settle into a slash—"is their captain. And will remain their captain until my father is rescued, or I am taken in his place. I swore by the Chain-breakers, same as any Reaper, that I would protect the Passengers. They deserve to know who protects them on the way to Horizon."

"But, Violet, I—" Gourd interjects, but I am already walking below deck, Moss scurrying to keep up.

"Their captain is giving the speech. Their captain is me. The conversation is over. Please grab your colored sands and meet me below deck as soon as you can." I wave over my shoulder, trying to sound confident but urging the ship forward even faster.

I don't want to be rude, but I also don't want to spend the entire journey back to Horizon debating who is and isn't captain.

I stand at the doorway to the lower decks of the *Moony*,

26

where the Passengers are gathered in wait. Moss stands at my side and holds himself a little higher as if he's the first mate of the ship now. He was so scared when I rescued him all those years ago, huddled in the very front row of the same crowded sleeping bunks where Dad gave the speech I'd seen him give a thousand times. And now Dad's gone, and I don't know where to start with rescuing him.

But I must. I will.

I descend into the belly of the ship. The Passengers huddle together, appearing almost like shadows in the candlelight.

In my mind, I rehearse the speech I've heard Dad recite so many times that I can practically hear his voice in my head telling the Passengers the story of our world.

5

Like most new Passengers, their eyes are wide with confusion, wrists and ankles raw where chains have bitten into skin. I make my way to the center of the room, slowly navigating through the whispering crowd. Eventually, I stand and scan them. They are us, our cousins tossed from ships and lost in the waves.

Lost, until now.

Gourd emerges from the crowd with the belt full of dyed sands that she always uses to accompany Dad's speeches. I used to love watching them, Gourd forming the sands into magnificent shapes of ships, storm clouds, and massive sharks while my father laid out the story of how our world came to be. All I ever talked about when I was Moss's size was how I wished to be the one telling that story. Now I'd give anything to have Dad back.

But I need to show Gourd that I can be captain. I need

her to know I can do this. I cough to pull the room's attention toward me. A tall, bald Passenger with scarred knuckles but tender eyes raises a fist, and slowly, the remaining whispers bleed from the room.

I give Gourd a look, and she grabs a handful of blue sand from her bag and brings it to her lips, whispering into it. The wind stirs around her hand, causing the sand to crash over and over like the waves of the tides. Excited whispers break out; I always forget that new Passengers have never seen magic before. But even I'm in awe of how the "water" sparkles in the dim light of the cabins.

I look at Gourd, whose eyes soften as she takes a dramatic pause, and then she reaches for a second dark bag at her waist. I watch the scattered black sand form into a fleet of massive ships that creep along the blue sand waves.

I take a deep breath and begin:

"Once, there were men who sought to chain the world—and so, they began with our ancestors. We were children of a gold continent, a place where the sun hung in the sky and the people stretched their Black, Black hands to drink in the warmth . . ." My voice quivers as the old story unspools from my memory and lips.

The eyes of the Passengers light up with their almost-memories. Sometimes, Moss tells me that he can remember the smells more than he can remember what he saw before the ocean, before everything changed.

As the story continues, and I talk of the Chainmakers, my voice bends into a growl. Whispers of hushed horror make their way through the crowd.

Gourd blows more black sand into the churning wind, and where there had been eight ships, now there are twenty. A child Passenger's mouth hangs wide open, awed but with terror in his eyes. Women's fists shake in the crowd, while others grasp the raw skin of their wrists.

". . . And the gods of the old world and the new seemed to weep, for they did not know how to undo what the world was becoming."

Silvered and gray sand floats on the enchanted winds and shapes itself into the clouds above the rotten ships, which seem to multiply with each new wave.

"But the gods are always listening . . ." One of the younger Passengers lets out a cheer, and I smile despite myself.

". . . And the gods looked to the tides and saw that the Sun People's prayers had turned to rebellion. And rebellion was a storm they could deliver."

The miniature storm clouds above the ships begin to condense, and the tides grow choppy as ship after ship sinks beneath the waves. Gourd's re-creation of the Storm at the Edge of the World captivates the surrounding souls.

Aboard the small ships, smaller figures spill from the lower decks and seize the wheel, tearing the sails down and helping more and more of their siblings, parents, children, and friends—all their people—from the hulls of the rotted boats. More young Passengers cheer as if, for even a moment, they've forgotten how much danger we are all in. I feel power flowing into my voice as I move into the next part of the story.

"The Sun People became their own Chainbreakers, the first Reaper captains, and their ships descended beneath the waves and found refuge in the Tides of the Lost, where we are now."

The blue sand parts as five ships float beneath the waves, symbolizing the first five Reaper captains.

". . . And the gods of the old world and the new were impressed with how the Chainbreakers cared for the dead as Passengers and siblings, not cargo or creatures only worth the work of their Black, Black hands."

In front of me, miniature Black figures descend from the ships on ropes, or dive down into the Depths, pulling silver people from the water.

Dad's last look at me flashes before my eyes, how strangely calm he seemed even as he fought to get to me. *Did his peace come from knowing he wouldn't make it back? Or that he could?*

I shake my head to clear the thought before I lose track of the story.

"And so, the Chainbreakers became the first Reapers of the Tides of the Lost. For the gods are always listening, and the gods were impressed. So the gods offered the first Reapers a gift."

Gourd undid the string of a third bag. It contained green sand, approximating the sickly light of the Children of the Shark.

"And a curse."

6

"And for a brief time, all was well on the Tides of the Lost . . . until the Chainmakers returned from below the water, mutilated by the hunger of an unbroken curse. They became the Children of the Shark, souls bound to hunt Passengers who hit the water. They became the Depths they dragged the souls down to. They became the teeth beneath the tide. And Chainmakers and Passengers alike were swallowed by an enormous shark, known as the Mother of Teeth."

A louder wave of murmurs sweeps through the crowd as some of the crew whisper among one another. "The Mother of Teeth is just a story, a myth to scare little children," says one crew member.

"I have a cousin who lives in Palm, and he saw a fin the size of a ship out on the water one night. How do you explain that?"

"Your cousin lives with the glass-sails on purpose. I have been to Palm, and I bet your cousin knows as much about sharks as he does about seasoning food."

A child Passenger with a small afro opens her mouth to ask a question. "Is that what those . . . things were?"

I nod, and a rumble goes through the room.

"The Children of the Shark"—I raise my hands to quiet the room—"are servants of the Depths, which are located in the ocean below us and where we cannot reach them."

"They took my niece." A woman near Gourd nearly spits the words out. "Do you intend to go free her, too?" She pauses, a disgusted look crossing her face. "Or will she become one of those things?"

I bite my lip before answering. "We don't know."

"What do you mean, you don't know?"

"I mean that I—"

"And why," the woman interrupts, voice rising, "are we hearing this from a child? Are you all that stands between us and those things returning?"

"That's enough." Gourd steps in, an edge to her voice. I clear my throat again, but the noise is growing, the focus is fraying. I stare at the gleaming tattoo on my forearm and feel my brow crease. I just want a moment alone, on my own.

Not yet.

I can feel the winds starting to whip harder around

me, and I take a deep breath to calm myself again before I explode.

My voice rings high and clear in a way I didn't know it could. "We are taking you to Horizon, to the Heaven we represent, and you will be safe there. I swear it to you. But you also do not have to stay there.

"Horizon is but one of Five Heavens," I close. "You may choose the one that suits you and be safe to make your new life there. There has never been an attack on one of the Heavens by the Pointers."

"And you're sure nothing can happen to us there?" another Passenger asks somewhere behind me.

"Yes, there's never been an attack on one of the Heavens," I repeat.

But there's never been a Reaper captain taken by Pointers until now.

A few more answers later, and I am out on the prow of the ship with Moss standing quietly at my side. The tides stretch off, dark and seemingly forever.

Everything is changing. The weight of losing Dad, of becoming captain, sits heavy on my chest. I know every puzzle has an answer, but that's no use if you can't find where to put the first piece.

I don't care what Gourd says, my father is alive. I can feel it. I can feel it in the tides and the breeze and in my own good bones. I feel it in the tattoo that makes me captain of this ship, his ship. I urge the *Moony* on faster toward Horizon, the salty air sharp in my nose.

True, a Reaper ship has never lost her captain. But that also means The *Moony* has never rescued her captain before, either.

But I will.

7

Normally, on days like today, when we'd arrive back in Horizon's port, Dad would wake early just to stand at the prow of the ship, eyes cutting through the mist, a small smile curling his mouth as the first lights found him.

This morning, though, I woke early for a different reason. Thin early light clings to the mast as I make my way to the back of the ship. I couldn't find sleep in the captain's cabin last night. I ate a little fish and rice but barely tasted it. Dad's face was on a loop in my mind, clunky and loud with nowhere to fit. I left Moss sleeping in our room, his almost-translucent little body curled in one corner of the bed, still and dreamless.

I need more information, and there is only one person to get it from before we arrive on Horizon and I have to face the council.

"You are late." The words come from above as a drawl, almost bored.

I climb the last rung of the ladder to the stern and can't help but grin at Sunshower's twin brother, Mooneye.

"That bowl may show you the tides but not what's right in front of you, old friend," I reply.

The man huddled over an ornate silver bowl chuckles dryly and looks up at me with a wry shake of his head. Where Sunshower's face is mapped by its laugh lines, Mooneye's is marked by a severe crease between his brows. The Tidewatcher's eyes scan my face quickly and then return to the bowl of water in his lap. In the water, I can see his upside-down face reflected, one eye a brown as rich as the soil in Root, the other scarred by a Pointer's blade, white as a pearl.

"My apologies, I suppose I should have foreseen this." Mooneye speaks without looking up. "Do . . ." He pauses. "Apologies again, Captain." Mooneye's voice is halting. "I need to get used to the new chain of command. What can I do for you?"

I wave off the apology and gesture for him to relax. Mooneye nods, raising his eyes toward me—something he and other Tidewatchers rarely do. They usually have their eyes on their water bowls, which show them the tides.

"You're the best Tidewatcher in all of the Five Heavens?" I ask.

"Naturally." Mooneye shrugs. "But, before you, um, ask, I have limits. Like anyone else."

I grimace, my subtle plan to ask a favor unspooling before my eyes.

"So you do know why I'm here."

"It felt safe to assume our new captain wonders where we might find the old one."

"I'm not here to ask about that." I semi-lie. "I want to know what you felt in the water when he disappeared. If he had drowned, you'd have felt him become a Passenger in the water, correct?"

Mooneye stiffens, his pearl eye narrowing at the bowl. "I would have . . ." His dull tone drags over each word. "It was a strange sensation. Like part of the water went missing. A space I couldn't see into. The captain—Virgil, I mean—he simply disappeared."

"Disappeared how?" I try to keep my voice calm, but my pulse is quickening.

"I wish I could summon more precise phrasing, Captain, but my brother's the wordsmith." A frown pulls the lines of Mooneye's face deeper. "But things have felt wrong on the seas recently. I can—I can see *something* moving sometimes with the Children of the Shark. A dull space, a quiet between them."

I strain not to roll my eyes. Mooneye says Sunshower is the wordsmith, and yet Mooneye is the one speaking in riddles.

"What do you mean, a quiet between them?"

Mooneye draws a finger along the surface of the water in his bowl. "Everything in the water around us—I see and feel it as I stare into this. I see Passengers and Pointers, I see the edge of the Depths from which the Children of the Shark emerge. I could stare into this bowl for a hundred years . . ." Mooneye pauses, drawing a deep breath, the salt clinging to the air around us. "And I would never run out of things to name, to see, to feel. But within the Depths, there is a quiet, a veil, I cannot penetrate on even my best day. When your father disappeared, it felt like that."

My chest sinks. I'd been hoping Mooneye might provide answers, but instead I'm left with even more questions.

I hear the wood of the ladder behind creaking with weight. Someone's coming.

"Mooneye, one last question—" I begin but not before Sunshower's head pops over the edge.

Sunshower's normal grin is gone this morning, and his frown deepens as he sees me. He is about to salute me, my first morning as captain . . . and maybe my last if the council has anything to say about it. But then the drums begin, and despite everything, I can see the far away lights of my city, my Heaven, our home.

Horizon, we have finally returned.

8

What I've always loved about Horizon is that you hear it before you see it. Alive or dead, Horizon is never shy about greeting you with a song. Rows of drummers line the shore, a choir of brightly dressed singers hold their notes, and the people of Horizon clap as I pull the *Moony* into port.

The hustle and calls of the market ring beneath the light of lanterns. Behind it all, the low-slung buildings and family homes have the salty, cinnamon smell of home. Drums boom in the distance to signal in our ship, and the laughs of stall merchants and Passengers alike spill over.

Everyone has come to welcome us home. Kwame of the Chainbreakers' Council and of Sand, the new chef of the Speared Squid, stand side by side, clapping in rhythm for the Passengers. Mekiba, a Passenger also from the Chainbreakers' Council, kisses the cheeks of those who embrace her, her silver locks framing her broad smile.

"Almost ready?" a warm voice coos at my shoulder.

"I'll be fine," I say to Sunshower, dusting off my clothes and wishing I wasn't about to reveal myself as the new captain while being both a kid and wrinkly from a long journey.

"You will be," Sunshower responds, clapping me on the shoulder. "Now, the key to all this will be not to look at the council members."

"Because they'll want to have a meeting, I bet, so better to avoid them so I can prepare," I cut in. I shrug, trying to seem like my pulse isn't banging so hard in my ears I can barely hear every other word.

"Well, I was going to say because I'm at your side, and a handsome uncle beats a balding bureaucrat any hour." Sunshower flashes a grin.

I laugh despite myself.

"But yes, also because they will want to meet, and they'll be less likely to try and, um . . . recast your position if—"

"If they don't think I was looking at them?" I ask. "How does that make sense?"

"You know," Sunshower mused, flagging Moss over to stand at my other side. "I don't fully understand it, either, but I don't see how it can hurt."

We both laugh, and Moss draws himself up to his full height before we step out behind Gourd and into the roar of the crowd.

Immediately, a hush falls over the questioning crowd, who had been so ready to greet my dad, the hero of Horizon. Moss slips his hand into mine.

Gourd slows her pace to get within earshot of our group at the back. "Violet, if the look on Kwame's face is any sign, we will need to go directly to the council chambers after this."

My stomach drops slightly, but also, what did I expect? How else are they going to react to the worst rescue mission ever?

The seven iron links that hang on the doors of the council chamber clink in the wind. Gourd stands stiffly, arms clasped behind her back, as we walk side by side as captain and first mate for the first time since the Children of the Shark took Dad.

"Now, when they make the call for the captain," Gourd says under her breath, boots clicking, "I think it might be best if I enter first."

I stop walking, staring hard at Gourd, who continues to explain.

"They will need to be, um, brought in slowly, regarding Virgil's . . . Well, we just need to bring them in slowly. They are . . . not used to the company of the young."

A little fire lights in my gut. It's one thing to think I may have to surrender the captaincy because I don't have my father's experience, but the idea of losing my chance to be there to rescue him sits sour in my throat.

"I think the element of surprise regarding who is and isn't the captain probably died when I stepped off the ship."

I shrug, trying to sound polite but walking faster toward the door.

"Violet, please, I know the council," Gourd says, flicking a bead of sweat from her brow. "They are very traditional. Help me help you to help them see reason, eh?"

I pause, considering. "We walk in together," I say finally as we arrive at the door.

Gourd shakes her head, casting her eyes upward before letting out a heavy sigh. "You know, you look way too much like your father when you are in the middle of telling me that you are going to do whatever you want to do no matter what I say. Has anyone ever told you that?" Gourd hides her mouth behind her hand to stifle a small, sad laugh.

"You, several times." I grin back, then pause. "Actually . . . it's a long list now that I think about it."

"Well, if that is going to be the case"—Gourd kneels and rolls up my sleeve so that the Mark of the Scythe is visible and glowing on my forearm—"you might as well look like a captain while you make the list longer."

9

The Chainbreakers' Council chamber shimmers as we enter, the scales of fish reflecting rings of soft green light. Ahead of me and Gourd, the seven council members each wear the ornate robes and gilded shark-tooth earrings indicating their position. The eldest, Nkosi Branch, opens her wrinkled eyes wide at the Mark of the Scythe on my forearm.

"Then it is true? Virgil has fallen to the Children of the Shark?" The last words slide out in a whisper, as if she is afraid the Pointers will hear.

Gourd nods stiffly, then tells the story to the council.

I can hear the waves lapping at the boards beneath our feet. The eyes of the Reaper council members are all heavy with sadness, Mekiba's especially. She is the first Passenger in the history of Horizon to bear the Mark of the Scythe. Her long braids shimmer like strings of pearls as she holds in silent sobs. Mekiba was captain of the *Moony* when my father first became a Reaper. I wish she would look at me, but every time I try to catch her eye, it causes every line in her weathered face to deepen.

I clear my throat to break the quiet. "I have something to say, as captain of the *Moony*." I pause, waiting for a response, but the council all wait patiently. I was expecting a bit more resistance. "The Children of the Shark have stolen my father. As his daughter, I have trained at his side, I have known what it means to be a Reaper and to protect our home and help other souls find home here as well."

I look around at the council, who all lean in intently. I straighten my shoulders, just as my father often did—does—trying to draw them in farther.

"Horizon's streets run full of Passengers who have been saved by the *Moony*, by my father, but today they are quiet. Silent. This act of aggression cannot go unanswered. And I—"

"Apologies, young one," says a council member to my left, thumbing a silver nose ring. "Our hearts are heavy with your loss, with our loss. Virgil has been our silver arrow, a fine captain. But I am not sure how exactly you mean to 'answer'? Wage war on the Depths? How can we wage war on a place we can't even reach?"

I should have known that adults wouldn't be able to stay quiet long enough for me to finish my point. I look back at Gourd, who looks like it's taking every ounce of willpower she has to remain still and not squeeze the bridge of her nose in frustration at all the noise.

"It'd be a foolhardy task if Virgil were still here, but to propose to do so *without a captain* is . . ."

A flare of anger surges through my body, and I feel the Mark of Scythe glow hot on my forearm. Windthreader magic, the wordless command that only comes with the Mark, swirls around me, tossing my locks in wild patterns around my face.

"I am not requesting a war," I rush to say, trying to cover up my outburst. "But the *Moony does* have her captain."

I stick my forearm out, the pale purple scythe glowing a violet as brilliant as my name. Mekiba squints down at me, a begrudging smile at the corners of her mouth that doesn't meet her sad, sad eyes. I take a deep breath and look back at Gourd one last time before I make her *really* mad.

"As captain, I am requesting the blessing of the council to mount a rescue mission to the Depths to retrieve him."

For a second, the room is so quiet that I wonder if I just imagined saying my big plan out loud. But the eyes of the council members are all shifting. Some stare at the glowing dome above them, and others look at me with pity in their eyes.

"Violet." Mekiba's voice is so quiet I almost don't hear her at first. "You are not here because we are going to try to wrest the captaincy from you."

My heart leaps in my chest; I thought I was definitely about to get confined to the shore.

"Honestly," rumbles Kwame, "I had raised some concerns as to whether it might be better for the young captain to rest a spell back here in Horizon. To lose Virgil so tragically . . ."

I fight to keep my face neutral, but internally I bristle at how even though I'm now captain, adults still speak of me as if I'm not right here. Not capable. Not—

"And I told Kwame," Mekiba interjects softly, "that the Violet Moon I know would not be kept off the *Moony* by anything."

I unclench my fists.

Mekiba smiles softly as she continues. "Violet Moon was born to be captain of the *Moony*. I've known it since Pearl was ripped away from us by that Pointer."

A collective sharp intake of breath overtakes the hall as I see the council members' eyes go distant, likely remembering my mother's candle boat ceremony. I wasn't at her funeral because after Mom was murdered, I stole her sword belt from her bag and snuck aboard the *Moony*. Mekiba had been the one to find me eventually, the sword belt so big around my hips it jingled from my hiding place.

It sits fast across my waist now, though. I run my hands along the old leather, fingers grazing the well-worn hole where Mom had fastened the belt two notches away from my own.

"We are not in the business of forcing the hand of anyone, but you will remain under the very close supervision of Gourd. And in times of crisis, she is to be considered as much of an authority as you. Furthermore . . ."

I cock an eyebrow, worried now about what's on the other side of that pause.

"The council cannot approve a doomed mission. Your rescue mission request is denied."

All the sound rushes out of the room. But then I stand straight and speak in my most confident voice.

"I would like to know when this decision was made. How soon do you imagine it will be before word spreads like a plague through the market? The Children of the Shark now take living captives. They have taken our captain and my father. Let me be the one to bring him back."

"You would risk the only ship Horizon has, our only means of rescuing Passengers, for one man, who we have to presume is . . . ?" A councilor next to Mekiba trails off.

"My father is alive," I growl. "And I would risk it for my father."

"And do you"—Mekiba leans forward in her seat—"know the difference between what you ask as a captain and what you ask as a daughter?"

The question punches the wind from my chest. Tears prick my eyes, but I blink them back and say flatly, "I know the difference. I have been training for this role my whole life. What I don't know is why this council refuses to even discuss trying to—"

"There is no evidence that anything but the Children of the Shark can travel between the Depths and the Five

Heavens." Councilor Kwame's deep voice rolls across the chamber. "We all loved Virgil—"

There it is again, everyone talking about Dad in past tense as if he is already gone. *Why is everyone so ready to push forward as if everything is fine?*

"You don't know he's dead," I say under my breath.

But either nobody hears me, or nobody cares. I look at Gourd, whose jaw is set in a hard line like she's bracing for a big wave. I scowl at everyone in the chamber.

"If I am not here to be stripped of my rank, and I am not here to rescue my father, then why—" I pause, reaching for something formal and captain-like, and ask through gritted teeth, "What honor brings me before the council?"

An uneasy look passes between the council members before Mekiba finally speaks. "The council thought it best to involve you in the planning for Virgil's candle boat ceremony."

A cold feeling passes over my skin, and I feel so lonely. I am on my own. The council will be no help. They do not know if Dad is truly dead, but still they have decided he is already gone.

→ 10 →

A quiet spreads over the chamber as the council looks to me for a reaction. I fight to keep my face still, but I can feel my mouth turning into a grim slash.

"Violet?" Gourd nudges me, a note of concern heavy on her tongue.

"You want . . . You want to plan his funeral? Right now?" I can hear my voice, but my mind is far from my body, a cold stealing up my arms. "He hasn't even been gone a day! And you're ready to pronounce him dead?" My voice is rising as another councilor cuts in.

"Your father was a hero, to Horizon, to this council, to all of us."

"Apparently, not enough of a hero for you all to even *try* to let me bring him back."

"Violet," says Eniola, a little steel in her voice now as I keep stepping out of place. "You father was your father, and yours alone. But he was also a symbol, like any other Reaper captain. This Heaven owes him an unpayable debt, but that debt cannot be paid in grief alone."

I open my mouth, but Gourd squeezes my shoulder hard and subtly shakes her head.

Eniola continues, "Nor can it be paid in doomed missions to the edge of our world. The people cannot lose two captains in a row. And what of the Passengers who will hit the water in the days to come? What will they do with one less ship to protect them?"

"I know what it is to lose someone you love to the Children of the Shark. " Kwame's low growl of a voice slides into the pause. "My cousin, Rice, died in Crest. He was a Windthreader on a mission near the edge of the Depths. They tried to find a way to see past the Fang Waves. They failed, and it cost me the last of my family.

"With this loss, came deep pain. I would have set fire to the tides without question, if only I knew how. But his time had come, and he had no desire to stay as a Passenger." A sad smile spreads briefly over Kwame's face before sliding away.

"To him, the space beyond, with the ancestors and the unknown. That was also an adventure."

"For we know death . . ." Eniola says solemnly.

"Is never the end," the rest of the councilors respond.

I join their chorus and feel a lead weight settle over my heart. I instinctively feel the guilt of agreeing.

"The candle boat ceremony"—Kwame's voice shakes slightly—"is a tradition, without which I would have had no light, only despair. The people of Horizon, they need that for your father. It is a space for us to move on, move forward, celebrate those who have left us and where they are headed."

I look around at the council, and they have that look on their faces that Dad used to wear when his mind was made up. I feel my shoulders sink.

I used to think being captain would mean I could finally make my own decisions—I never imagined my captaincy would begin like this. I take a deep breath, and it tastes like defeat.

"Fine. We will have the ceremony. Sunshower will be the Archer."

"We had hoped that—" comes a wizened voice from my right.

But I repeat, "Sunshower *will* be the Archer. That is what Dad would have wanted, and as captain of the *Moony*, I—"

"Actually." Eniola's face softens with a bit of relief. "We had hoped that you would select Sunshower."

I nod, and my mind is a hundred paces from my body. But this time it's not just the heaviness of grief.

If Crest has run missions to the Depths before . . .

At the door, I say goodbye to Gourd and tell her I am heading off to the market, as I need time to think. Gourd looks too tired to be skeptical and pulls me into a rib-cracking hug. Then she turns on her heel and is gone, and I'm standing alone at the front door of the council chamber.

Well, not just me.

"So," I say to the air, then stomp my boot quickly three times. "How much of that did you catch?"

Moss pops his little shaved head out from behind one of the columns in front of the chamber. His mouth is a perfect flat line in the middle of his pale, glowing face. He looks like he could be the moon's son.

"Not a whole lot; that council chamber wood is thick." Moss frowns further. "Are we . . . really not going to go after him?"

I give Moss a long look. His small shoulders are slumped toward his chest. He's the heaviest with sadness I've ever seen him. I wonder if that's how I looked to Eniola or Gourd. I give Moss a winning smile and cock my head back toward the market.

"Of course we are, but first," I call back over my shoulder, already on my way toward the market, "we're going to grab ourselves a squid who knows more than he lets on."

⟝ 11 ⟞

Ordinarily, the streets of the market in Horizon dance with the scent of fried fish and gluttonous laughter. Children tug at long colorful skirts, pleading with their mothers to buy them a treat that a merchant's Windthreading magic dangles above the crowd. Everywhere is the hustle and clatter of hundreds of lives and souls. If Sunshower were at my side, someone would be trying to sell him an ornate bowl that Mooneye would say is not only ugly but unnecessary.

I love it on a normal day, but today is not a normal day. Instead, the covered stalls are bared like wooden ribs, the sellers do not call and haggle, and the people buying produce imported from Root do so in hushed voices as if they fear the sharks already beneath their feet may come for them.

The people of Horizon are quiet because they do not believe their lives will continue to be safe. Eniola is right about one thing—the streets understand that they have lost someone irreplaceable. And with this loss, with Virgil's capture, the world we knew has changed.

"So run me through this one more time." Moss wears a quizzical look, his brow bunched in a great knot between his thin eyebrows.

"Well, Phase One is for you to undo that little mountain in the middle of your face."

I tap Moss between the eyes playfully and try to grin, but his expression tells me the smile doesn't reach my eyes. Turns out you can lie to the council, but you can't lie to the people who really know you.

"All right." I lower my voice as we pass by a depressed shopkeeper, who wordlessly offers me a beaded bracelet the color of seawater, then recognizes who I am and puts it back down. "In the meeting, the council said that they wouldn't approve a mission to the Depths to rescue Dad, right? *But*, they never said anything about using the *Moony* to track down someone who *did* survive the mission."

Moss's eyes go wide, then his brow furrows twice as deep.

"Someone survived . . . that?" A little shiver passes over his frame as we hang a right down an alleyway that smells of old shrimp.

"No. Well, maybe. Maybe Kwame's cousin didn't make it, but I bet we can find someone who did. You just gotta know who to ask." I high-step over the bones of a fried cod. "That's what we're on the way to find out."

A drab shopkeeper halfheartedly flags us down to look at dolls that dance and each act out a small story if a Wind-threader tells it. I used to have a doll that performed the origin story of the Reapers of Root finding the Star-Drenched Baobab, but I stopped playing with it after Mom was killed. The dolls shuffle briefly in the wind before collapsing like sticks.

Moss doesn't respond, so I continue as we turn toward the crown jewel of Horizon's market: the Speared Squid. The mahogany building leans to one side like a tired uncle col-lapsing into a chair. Normally, like Horizon, it is a place that you hear before you see.

"We're on our way to see Sand," I say, referring to the chef who greeted us earlier when we docked the *Moony*.

"What would a line cook from Palm know about a dan-gerous mission to the Depths?" asks Moss.

I smirk just a little despite myself. "An ordinary line cook? Nothing. But a spy disguised as a line cook, who also happens to make the best grilled squid in the Five Heavens? Well, he just might be able to help us."

One late night between missions, Dad had told me that many years ago, the Heaven of Palm began the Ministry of Historians. It started out with a bunch of history nerds collect-ing the stories of people's lives, but as the years progressed, the Historians became Palm's greatest resource for keeping track of the movements and political structures of the other Heavens.

I told Dad they sounded more like a society of super-gossips than spies, and he had laughed so hard he nearly choked on his okra. I snort at the memory.

What a horrible way that would be to go: death by vegetable, I think. Then I feel a pang in my stomach at the word *death*.

"Anyway, I just feel it, like, in my bones. Nah," I revise, "I feel it in my spirit; if there's a survivor of the Depths, Sand will know where to start. So just follow my lead, and y'know, don't give away that we know his true nature. He's not a very good spy. The first week he was here, I had noticed the San-kofa tattoo between his fingers. Real amateur stuff honestly, but I think he thinks he's being subtle."

Moss stares at me in wonder, then a troubled expression passes over his face like a storm cloud. "You know I'm no good with secrets."

"Then"—I pull the doors wide with a grunt—"*definitely* follow my lead."

The inside of the Seared Squid is less crowded than usual, and a hush falls over the space as I step inside. The last time I was here, I wasn't exactly invisible. After all, I was the captain's daughter. But back then, people stared so they could raise a glass to Dad, some to thank him for saving them, eager to tell him the stories of the lives they had built with his help. And I would beam, looking at him greeting them all. My dad, father to half the city.

But now folks were straight up staring at me. I was—I

am—the captain now. And even though it's only been a few hours since we docked, the word has spread like wildfire.

Well, there is no time for fear. Only answers.

The scent of fried swordfish wafts out of the kitchen as I give a polite nod to the onlookers at their long tables and take a seat. Right on cue, out comes Sand to greet us. The scent of smoke clings to him, and sweat pours in little rivers from the top of his head all the way down the backs of his arms.

"Greetings to the newest captain," Sand croons, reminding me to not trust the perfumed way every *S* seems to slither from his mouth. "You honor my humble establishment with your presence, Captain. I can't resist the desire to sit for a spell with you, if you would permit it."

I shoot a lighthearted told-you-so look at Moss and gesture to the open seat between us. Moss shrugs, then plops down in the seat next to me.

"Before I say anything else," Sand continues, close enough that I can smell the shrimp on his breath, "I must express my condolences. Your father was a hero."

"He still is," Moss pipes up, his brow creased.

"Ah, my apologies, my apologies. I meant no offense . . ."

Sand begins to push himself back from the table, but I send Moss a warning look and slide my boot behind the leg of Sand's chair to halt it.

"There's no need for"—I swallow hard—"apologies. If anything, I am grateful for your consideration at this difficult time."

I wrestle a soft smile onto my face and see the lines of Sand's face relax.

"Captain Virgil was a graceful man. I am humbled to find that it is a familial trait."

"But of course." I nod as food I don't remember us ordering is brought to the table.

And not just any food, a squid seared in a special cocktail of herbs, the namesake of the restaurant. The tentacles glisten with sizzling oil, the seasoning studding the crisped skin with charred little diamonds.

Sand really must be curious about me being the new captain if he's pulling out all the stops. Maybe best to give him a little something more to be curious about.

"Honorable chef, you flatter us. I had no idea that you had spent time in Shard, researching their delicacies like this fine dish. We are actually plotting a mission there ourselves."

Sand fights to keep his face neutral, but the sweat polishing the top of his head increases. Of course, Shard doesn't have any special dishes; their people are all a bunch of overeager stormheads. But Sand doesn't know that I know that. He doesn't know that I'm quickly pushing him toward giving up his secrets.

"Well actually, I picked up this little ditty from the good people of Root."

"Root?" I pump a little enthusiasm into my voice. "Really? That must have been fascinating. And you went there right after your time in Crest, if I'm correct?"

Sand draws a sharp intake of breath.

By the ancestors, with behavior that obvious, I have no idea how nobody else has noticed Sand is a spy.

"Oh well, you would be mistaken, Captain," Sand adds hurriedly. "I wouldn't know anything about Crest. The Fang Waves are, um . . . unacceptable to my disposition. I'm too prone to seasickness for the Crest Reapers' daredevil culture. I'm, hmm, a creature of the kitchen."

Moss rolls his eyes. "You're a creature of whispers and rumors."

"What did you say?!" Sand splutters.

I glare at Moss, who bites his lip. But the game is already up. Sand pushes himself back from the table.

"My apologies, Captain, I meant only to come out for a moment, and it appears I—"

I clamp my palm down atop his hand to hold the man still.

"It appears you have been to Crest, especially since all cooks from Root season their fish in diagonal lines. Only Reapers from Crest season in diamond patterns, and only other Reapers know that. You haven't just been to Crest; you sailed on their ships." I stare into Sand's eyes, which are wet and amber colored like the rest of him. "I think, given your history"—I pry his fingers apart and tap the second knuckle where he has hidden the Sankofa bird insignia of the Palm Ministry of Historians—"you know where I might start looking for something I need: information on a certain mission from Crest to the Depths, to be exact."

Sweat pours in great streams off Sand's arms. "And if," his voice creaks, barely above a whisper, "I were to say that what the captain seeks cannot be found?"

"I would notify the Horizon council that you're a spy, to begin with. Maybe they'd send you back to Palm. *Maybe* that's all the punishment they'd dole out."

Tension bristles along the Historian's arm.

"But perhaps we might avoid that . . . *unpleasantness*? For example, if you were to answer my simple questions about that rumored mission,"—I pause, milking the quiet as long as I can—"maybe I could forget what I know about you."

Sand's expression hardens and melts three times over. His mouth moves like a trapped animal, thrashing between smile and frustration, victory and defeat, before finally he opens it, shoulders slumped. I am at the edge of victory; I can taste it—

CRASH.

An enormous roar explodes from the kitchen, and before I can blink, Sand has pulled his hand back from mine and is hustling off to the kitchen, promising to return in a few moments.

I bite my lip.

So close.

"I'm sorry, Vi—"

I wave Moss off, eyes still hard, focused on the entrance to the kitchen.

"Everyone here is still staring. We can't afford to look

frustrated, or people will get suspicious. We have to wait for him to come back."

But when Sand comes back, he does not shine with sweat. He does not tremble at being found out. He is dry as a bone. He sits and says nothing.

That is because it is not truly him. Just a trick.

He is only the slight whistle of the wind as the wind-figure he has sent out to pretend to be him collapses into nothing more than a pile of painted sand.

— 12 —

My pulse slams in my ears as Moss and I burst through the doors of the Speared Squid. My empty stomach sloshes, but there's no time to lose as we scan the street and find Sand nowhere.

Moss turns to me with wide, apologetic eyes. "What do we do, Vi?"

"He can't have gone far. So you go high"—I make a basket by interlacing my fingers and eye the roof—"and I'll stay low."

Moss salutes and steps into my hands as I launch him to the rooftop. He gives a whistle, and I chase the sound, boots pounding hard against the wood. I feel the Mark of the Scythe tattoo drumming against my forearm, growing warmer as the chase continues. Moss whistles from up high again, and I snap my head up just in time to see a gleaming bald spot whip around the corner. I slow my heartbeat, breathe deep, and turn the corner into the more crowded main market.

On the main walkway, sellers hawk their wares and call out to friends and neighbors. Tailors swing large, patterned flags and dashikis, and I see with a pang the white saronas in preparation for Dad's candle boat ceremony.

I keep pressing through the crowd, one eye trained on the roofs where Moss moves silent as a star. Dad said once that he knew Gourd was his best friend because he could trust her to be his eyes when his faltered. I don't think I knew what he meant until now.

Finally, as Sand attempts unsuccessfully to disguise himself by haggling with a shopkeeper over a melon, I spot what I am looking for. I turn up the collar of my jacket and slide into a booth on the opposite side. The shopkeeper is a kindly woman from Palm, a lucky gap between her two front teeth, each with a gold cap and tiny pearl bright as the moon. Two-Moons smiles at me as I glance over my shoulder, attempting not to be seen chasing after a respected business owner on my first full day as captain. We haggle briefly before I surrender a few coins to her, and she hands me a small bag. I turn around to see Sand, almost in slow motion, drop the melon he has just bought. Mouth agape, he stares up at Moss on the tarp directly above him.

Sand sprints, slipping slightly on the melon before launching himself into the gasping and scandalized crowd. Moss gives chase from above, while I jog behind and dip my hand in the bag at my side. I begin to mutter into my palm, panting between the words of the Windthreader spell.

"*Little friend, fast friend, friend of a thousand stories and songs, be my palm of mirrors, give hands to your stories, and let them reach for the listener; I will let what you make wear my face.*"

The painted sands swirl a miniature storm in my palm, then the churning sands curl in the air like a cloud and disappear.

"Vi, he's headed left!" Moss bellows, all subtlety now abandoned.

I bank left, nearly turning my ankle. A small roof extends over a doorway, so I increase my speed, the wind baying at my heels nearly lifting me with each step until I leap and haul myself up onto a roof of my own and survey the scenery.

"He's . . . fast . . . for an old . . ." Moss wheezes as he runs over next to me, hands on his knees. "Don't we need to catch him before he, like . . . gets to the boats?"

I can almost see the harbor behind him. I tousle his hair, my little brother, the only person I can trust now. "We already have."

Moss is about to argue, when I turn my eyes to the sky and smirk, seeing a cloud of painted sand descending not far from where Sand is headed.

"You never told me Gourd taught you the wind-figure spell." Moss's smile cracks his face in two.

"Technically, she didn't, and I won't lie—" I begin hustling across the rooftops, Moss not far behind. "The wind-figure is probably going to be pretty ugly. But it's just a first draft."

But first draft or not, it does the trick. As it comes face-to-face with Sand, he stops short, and his eyes light up with fear. He desperately turns and turns and turns, but each time, the sandy clone rises into the sky and re-forms in front of his eyes.

I can feel beads of sweat running down my forehead as I keep one eye concentrated on the spell and the other focused on not falling off the roof.

Finally, Sand turns a corner and finds himself at a dead end, right below us. I hurl my knife and pin the edge of his simple black dashiki to the wall behind him. I feel a little of my strength leave me as I call the wind-figure Violet back to me and advance on Sand.

"Well, turns out we're going to have to do this the hard way." I clear my throat. "Enough running. Where is the ship?"

"What ship?" Sand coughs, drawing his fist across his mouth.

Rage flares in my veins, and I step closer until I am in his face.

"Maybe all this cloak-and-dagger has made me unclear. Let's try again." I smile, baring my teeth. "My father has been stolen by the Children of the Shark. You have information on a ship that attempted to sail to the Depths. I am running low on patience and even lower on time, so I'm going to ask again . . . What do you know?"

And then Sand lets out a bitter laugh. And another. And another. I feel my fists clenching and the Mark of the Scythe glowing a ravenous, deep purple on my forearm.

Finally, he speaks. "You're searching for a phantom. A

lone survivor from the mission, a super-soldier from Shard doing research with the Reapers of Palm. And I can't help you find him."

"Who is this man? Research on what?" I grab the collar of Sand's clothes and pull him even closer until I can count the pores on his broad face.

"Nobody knows. I never even saw him. Just reports from the other Historians, but they're all nonsense. Fables about a boy made of wings, a super-soldier who returned."

"He must have a name." Moss crosses his arms, trying to look tough.

"Dirge. His people, the Reapers of Shard, called him Dirge." Sand laughs bitterly once more, then looks me directly in the eye. "Boy of Wings, Doom of the Depths. But none have seen him; he's been gone for years. I doubt he ever existed."

I feel the dashiki slip from my fingers as Sand continues to speak, a cruel smile on his face. "You've chased me across half of Horizon over a bedtime story, a legend for small children." He nods at Moss. "You may as well take your knife back, Captain; I've answered your questions. Now you agree to forget who I serve, and we do not cross paths again."

I yank my knife free, my mind still spinning with the new information. What kind of strange riddle was this? A boy made of wings in a world without birds?! It was nonsense.

Sand straightens himself, an indignant look on his face as he begins to walk back toward his restaurant.

"I really did mean my condolences, and I still do. But, Captain, you can sail from one end of the Tides of the Lost to the other. You can visit every Heaven and chase a hundred Historians and beg the wind for guidance. But you will never find Dirge. He's even more of a ghost than your friend here."

— 13 —

We walk the remainder of the way back home in silence, Sand's riddle ringing in both our minds. It just doesn't make any sense. How can a survivor just have disappeared? Is Shard hiding him? How could those storm-frenzied dye-heads actually have kept a secret as enormous as a mission to the Depths? They don't even believe in inside voices!

I suck my teeth and spit onto the ground as Moss and I round the corner to our place. It isn't much because it doesn't have to be; most of our lives are spent on the *Moony*, where we belong. So even though Moss and Dad and I all have beds here, it's more of a storage locker than a home. Still, I don't feel right sleeping in the captain's quarters tonight. And I need some space from Gourd and everyone else to try to puzzle through what Sand could have meant and what to do next.

When I open the door, the air smells stale. I swing my arms to fan out the room. I swipe the dust off our kitchen table and reach in a small urn to grind up some glow powder to give the room some more light. Moss is still standing in the doorway, the light from outside nearly swallowing his form.

"Moss, you coming in?" I jab my head at his favorite seat while I look for something to wipe my hands on.

Moss nods but doesn't say anything, so I keep trying to shuffle the house into something like order. Great tomes and maps are spread everywhere. I groan involuntarily. Dad was always insistent that I learn how to read maps even though eventually I'd get to learn from the best Tidewatcher in the Five Heavens and maps are annoying and the dust makes me sneeze.

I drag a finger along the choppy lines west of Horizon: the Fang Waves, turbulent waters only the daredevil Reapers of Crest are experienced in navigating and rescuing Passengers from. I've always wanted to go. Dad said the Fang Waves were better seen than felt, but I just think that's because Mom was from Crest. That's why I've never been west of Moonpoint Harbor. Dad would always change the subject when I'd ask if we could go.

I used to think he was holding me back, but I feel my heart skip a beat as my hand passes over a spot on the map near where Dad disappeared.

Dad and I used to sit with these maps for hours. I wish he'd told me that when you lose someone you love, sometimes they take a whole part of the map with them.

I sniffle and roll up the map, tucking it into my pocket,

when I hear a muffled gasp from across the room. I look up from the map-covered desk to see Moss doubled over in his seat.

"Moss!" I splutter, dropping the maps and rushing to his side. "What's wrong, buddy? Are you okay? Did Sand do something to you?"

"No, it's—" Moss gasps between heaves and sobs that seem to vibrate his entire body.

"Moss, I can get the healer. I can—" I offer, brain spinning through a list of who to call for help.

~~Dad?~~ *Gourd? Mooneye?* ~~Dad?~~ *Sunshower?* ~~Dad?~~

"No, I've done enough." Moss's voice is so small, like the pop of a lit candlewick.

"What does that mean?" I say, holding his bony shoulders and fighting to keep my voice calm.

Moss takes a rattling breath to steady himself, his form growing opaquer in the dim light of the glow powder. "I've been trying to keep it in, because, because—" Another sob shakes his body. "It's just all my fault. All of it. You wouldn't have to be captain; you'd still have a fa—"

"Who said that was your fault?" My voice is soft.

"Nobody, I guess. Not with their words. It's just, we've never been here without—I don't know, Vi; it's all my fault." Moss shrugs, becoming somehow even smaller as he slouches into himself.

"I don't think that!" I offer, mouth twisting with guilt. "If anything, it's my—"

"But if I hadn't tried to help . . ." Moss interrupts. "If I hadn't gotten in the way . . . If I hadn't fallen off the side . . ."

I bite my lip, Dad's face flashing behind my eyes at the memory. And then a second memory, from here in this house actually. Not of the day my mother died, but of a day and a half later, when I was told what happened by Gourd and Dad. When the ship docked, I hadn't gone to greet it like everyone normally does. I'd finally solved a puzzle box that Mom had left behind as a challenge, and I was determined that it be the first thing she saw when she came in.

To hear Mekiba or Kwame or Dad tell the story, my mother, Pearl, was the fiercest Reaper fighter in all of Horizon, maybe even all the Five Heavens. But after she had me, she really struggled with feeling so far from the tides. They were only supposed to be gone a few days, according to Gourd. But on the second day of the journey, one of the smaller commercial ships that brought food and supplies from Root to Shard was attacked, and Mom had leapt off the side of the *Moony* onto the little ship to fight off the Pointers ten, then fifteen at a time. She battled them down to the last one, sword cutting broad silver arcs in the moonlight. When the last Pointer, a Great White twice her size, was sent skittering over the side of the boat, she thought she'd won. As she secured her rope to come back onto the *Moony*, the Great White pulled itself back onto the deck and stabbed her in the back. Just like that, I had no mother.

And now I can still hear how Gourd's voice was the

softest it had ever been when she explained that Dad had some terrible news he needed to share. I can still feel her arms around me, wrapped in her lavender scent as I sobbed. Ever since, Dad and Gourd don't talk much to me about Mom. They think I don't notice because I'm only twelve, but how could I not? They always say her name—Pearl—in a gentle whisper as if it were a fragile thing that would break if dropped.

I wonder if all through Horizon, people are saying Dad's name the same way.

I had made my way onto the *Moony* within days, where Mekiba found me because of the rattling sword belt now at my waist. Afterward, Dad agreed it was better to have me at his side rather than endlessly worrying if I was secretly some-where onboard, trying to protect him. It was a little strange at first, the whole crew looking at me with a mix of pride and sadness on their faces. Crew members would tell me stories about how I looked just like Mom, and after I learned to hold a practice blade, how I fought like her, too. It felt good to have something to do, someone to do it with. I hadn't been much older than Moss then. Maybe I can be one of those people for him now.

"*If the tides were turned to sugar, if all the rains led us home,*" I say in a singsong voice, and smile despite myself.

"What?" Moss is so confused, he temporarily stops crying.

I roll my eyes and smile bitterly. "It's something my dad said when I was little." I shift my voice to what honestly is an underrated impression of Dad.

"*If the tides were turned to sugar, if all the rains led us home, there would still be so many ifs to cloud the skies.*" I tut my tongue in that way he does that always made me roll my eyes when I was younger.

"*Sail forward, sail forward, the day provides enough clouds; breathe and focus on the stars you most wish to dance beneath,*" I finish, clearing my throat until I sound like me again.

"That was so pretty," Moss pipes in. "What does it mean?"

"Yeah, I think it means all you can control is the desire to keep going, y'know? Like, there will always be possibilities to freak out about even if everything goes the best it could. But honestly, I don't know—Dad loved weird poems." I groan at the thought of him dancing around the apartment, telling his stories.

"Loves," Moss corrects. "He's still out there, right?"

I blink hard, pushing aside my tears. My throat feels tight with shame to have slipped and spoken of my father in the past tense.

"You're absolutely right. One more reason this isn't your fault." I smile unconvincingly.

Moss tilts his head up as if in deep thought, then finally sighs and says, "He did like some weird, weird poems."

"You should have seen him with 'The Epics of Silvertongue.'"

I chuckle, "Gourd got him this special illuminated scroll of it, and it was all he talked about. For. A. Year."

We both laugh as I scan the shelves for the special carved handle of the script, and I instead spy something else. I lift the object gingerly, bring it down, and blow on it.

Moss looks quizzically at it. "What's that? It's hard to see in here."

I grin, running my hands over the edges of the object. "This was the first puzzle box that Dad ever made me."

I place the intricate wooden box in Moss's hands, and he weighs it as I light one of the candles at the map table.

"How do you open this thing?" Moss shakes the box near his ear before I snatch it up.

"Dad actually used to let me try to figure this one out before bed while he told me the story of the Archer with a Hundred Promises. The trick is that you can't look at the box head-on." I hold the box out flat in my palm and try to turn its sections; they won't rotate, each locked in place.

"Well, that seems like a badly made toy." Moss scrunches up his face.

"It would be, but Dad *loves* a teaching moment and . . ." I flip the toy so I hold the box diagonally. Each of the sections of the puzzle box slide a tiny bit down and into the central hinge. I spin the sections from memory until the box clicks open.

Moss claps, and I half grin, sealing the box back up.

"The point is that sometimes you have all the pieces you need; you just need to look at them from another angle to actually find the solution."

"That makes sense. I guess that's why you're—"

I cock my head. "Why I'm what?"

"Um"—Moss's eyes flit around—"so good . . . at puzzles?"

I keep an eyebrow cocked but muss his hair. "I guess you can keep whatever little rude observation you were about to make to yourself. And I'll just keep my plan to *myself*."

Moss claps his hand to his chest, indignant.

"Only kidding, but this puzzle box did get me thinking!" I tap my chin, pacing the room. "We could use some new perspective on this riddle from Sand if we're going to find Dirge."

"And where would we get that?" Moss's voice is creaky with skepticism.

"We go to the source. We set sail for Palm after the candle boat ceremony. For all we know, the soldier, Dirge, is no longer in Crest, so our best bet is asking Sand's Historian friends in Palm if they have any more information on the soldier's whereabouts. We'll tell Gourd and the crew we're there for a day or two to take on supplies, and we'll find our way into the Ministry of Historians' secret hideout. Once we find the information we need about how to navigate to the Depths, we'll convince Gourd and the Council to let us go on the mission."

"Okay." Moss nods slowly as if tasting the words. "I feel like you said that as if it is very simple, but—"

"Oh, it definitely won't be, but I don't see another option." I bare the glowing Mark to Moss, the purpled light playing across his face like starlight.

"You're the only person I can trust this plan with, Moss. Because you are his family, too." I clap my hand on his shoulder. "Moss Moon."

Moss's head snaps up at the last part, a broad grin splitting his smoky face in two. Reapers take on the last name honorific of their ship, that they might always carry it with them regardless of the tide or shore they find themselves on.

"We must move quietly and quickly if we're going to find Dirge and save Dad. Are you with me?" I extend my arm, and barely a second passes before he clasps it with one hand, a bold look in his eye.

"I am with you, Captain."

"Good, then we ought to go to bed. We have the candle boat ceremony in the morning," I mutter.

"All right," Moss concedes, sitting back down. "Can you show me how to open the puzzle box again first? It's going to keep me up thinking about it."

I chuckle and hand the polished oak and mahogany box to him.

"Well, while you figure it out, I'll tell you the story I heard when I was a little one trying to open it."

Moss's face brightens as he settles in to hear the story while carefully inspecting the box. I sit at his side and run my fingers through his tight curls—a little field of fists—before beginning the story.

— ✦ 14 ✦ —

"There once was an Archer, name now lost to the wind, who set out to hunt the dark from the sky. He was the greatest Archer in all the Five Heavens. He could pluck the string of his bow in Horizon, and the winds would carry his arrow to his target in Shard. He and his crew hunted beneath turbulent skies that glimmered in the moonlight, searching for rare fish and creatures not yet heavy with names. Into all this, the Archer built a good life, until one day one of his men, a Passenger, came to him and asked if the Archer knew the way to the ancestors.

"The Archer did not know, and so he asked the man, *Where are the ancestors you seek to find your way back to?* And the man did not know; he only knew that he had watched the moon grow dimmer, and he yearned deeply to be elsewhere. The Archer promised a hundred times that he would use his hunting skills to find his way to where the ancestors lay their heads so the man might know peace.

"They sailed the tides until silver hair began to wind through the beard of the Archer. The moonlit brother who sought his kin stepped to the Archer and said, *Brother, I think the ancestors do not mean to be found; only joined.* The Archer did not understand what he meant, and so the moonlit brother threw his arms wide beneath the inky sky. *I wish to be everywhere, as they are. Not in a single place that can be found, but in the sound of everything. Ancestor on the breeze, ancestor in the curl and kiss of the tide, ancestor in the juice of the fruit running down the sides of a child's mouth, ancestor in the moonlight, ancestor in the stars that have not yet reached us. Can you understand now?*

"And the Archer did, so he commanded that their ship dock on the shores of Root.

"Beneath the pitch-dark sky, the Archer and his remaining family dressed themselves and the moonlit brother in the scales of specterfish so that he might see his friends glowing on the shore he was leaving. The moonlit brother sat in the boat with one candle to light his way. The Archer trained his bow to the sky, and with each arrow that sailed into the clouds, a star revealed itself. And the light of the hunted stars danced along the skin of the moonlit brother as his friends sang and called his name. The skies shook with his praise as the Archer loosed one hundred arrows, and each star fulfilled his promise.

"The moonlit brother looked to the stars and let go as he dissolved into the air to meet the ancestors and find that he had become the rush of the tide and the flare of the new-found stars, the soil beneath his friends' feet and the wind their singing flew upon. He had become an ancestor; he had become everything and everywhere."

On the morning of my father's candle boat ceremony, there is not peace to be found as there was for the moonlit brother. I wake and find my throat raw as if I'm choking on a flame. Gourd escorts me to the edge of the ceremony with her at my left and Moss clinging to my right hand. I am far from my body, my mind already aboard the *Moony*. I try not to feel the hundred pairs of eyes on my skin as I straighten the edge of my sarona and the ceremonial earrings clatter at either side of my head.

I need to look like a captain, not a daughter, I remind myself. *The city needs its protector. Convince the people that you are her.*

I swallow hard and stomp forward as we march slowly to the edge of the harbor. People line the rooftops and streets, everyone draped in white. My people, a pretty constellation spread over every building, watching us pass. Some say small thank-yous, others fight to choke their tears down as I walk by without meeting their eyes.

A captain, not a daughter.

The choir begins as Gourd places a hand on my shoulder. It feels nice, even if Gourd's face is chiseled stone as the

82

song builds. Kwame of the council is at the front, stomping a percussive rhythm that is picked up by a group of performers behind him. The song builds in strength as the crowd joins in. I know it's my turn, my time to complete the ceremony. But now, in the swell of the song, my legs are rooted, two spindly trees holding up my body.

Gourd squeezes my shoulder, and I look up to see her eyes soften as she looks at me. Her mouth is slightly open as if she is about to say something, but she just purses her lips and reassuringly squeezes my shoulder again.

I nod, take a shuddering breath, and walk forward along the dock toward the empty boat waiting at its end.

The boat has been painted a white that rivals the crescent moon above. My father's name is threaded now within the song, a call and response that has the air buzzing. I sneak a look two docks over to see the *Moony*, dark wood almost drinking in the moonlight; the only thing not dressed for a funeral. I'd give anything not to be here, not to be seen, not to be the most important part of a funeral for a man I don't think is dead; for the only family I can still save.

A captain, not a daughter, I think one last time as I kneel at the edge of the dock, summoning my Windthreader magic to gently press the boat out into the waiting tides. A silver candle is its only passenger.

I stand alone at the end of the dock, watching the boat, a single white speck in the otherwise black ocean. The choir's voices braid gorgeously, honey and twilight to the percussion of so many more stomping and shouting his name. I fight back a sour laugh. How Dad would have loved this, his whole Heaven turned to an orchestra for him, and he's the only one who isn't present.

Sunshower needs only one fire arrow to light the candle, the flame a lone beacon as the tides and my own spell carry the boat farther and farther out. I swallow and find the fire in my throat, a rage that spills into my blood until the music fades and I am standing alone thinking only two thoughts: *You should still be here* and *I will steal you back; I swear it on every star in the sky.*

— 15 —

"Ah, Captain Violet," Mooneye croons from the crow's nest of the *Moony*, eyes still glued to the ornate bowl in his hands. "I assume you are here to check if we are prepared to set sail for Palm."

All we have to do is make it to Palm, dock for a day or two, and discover where all the secret Historians are hiding. Palm is bustling with people, so maybe we'll even find Dirge hiding there. It's where I'd go if I was trying to lay low from . . . Well, that's another question: What would a super-soldier need to *hide* from?

"Actually, Sunshower tells me everything is ready to go. I'm here because I was wondering if you would teach me more about Tidewatcher magic?"

"Well, well," Mooneye says dryly, a thin smile reflected in the waters. "You really are ducking Gourd."

My eyebrows nearly fly off my forehead before I cough and try to fix my face. Gourd has been strangely . . . quiet since the candle boat ceremony. When I said the *Moony* was sailing for Palm to stock up on painted sands, she barely blinked and asked me to relieve her of the deck so she could go and straighten some of her personal effects.

"I don't blame you." Mooneye taps the space across from him with his foot. "Gourd is my favorite storyteller but my least favorite person to be lectured by. Anyway, take a seat and get ready to learn some real magic."

"Is the wind that moves the ship not magic?" I smirk, sitting and placing my hands at the edge of the bowl.

"Parlor tricks." Mooneye shrugs. "Tidewatching is an ancient art. It's not even named properly, if you ask me."

"I don't know about that. You kinda spend a lot of time looking into that bowl."

Mooneye makes a clicking noise with his teeth. "Ah yes, I see that, like your mother, you believe yourself to be the first person who has ever told me that joke."

Ouch. Tough, but fair.

"As I was saying, Tidewatching isn't the best name for it. The true artists of this magic do not simply watch the waters, they feel them. It's a form of knowing that, once you learn it, you will never be without it. Now, are you prepared to begin, my captain?"

Mooneye offers a rare flash of eye contact, and his one gray pupil is warm like rising daylight. His mooned eye bristles beneath with blue energy.

I nod and stare into the bowl. I search for the balanced

space that allows me to urge the *Moony* forward. I do not look up as the city is swallowed by its mists; I watch my own face. And then my vision reaches deeper, past my reflection on the water and down until all I hear is the tide in the bowl. The crash of the waves swells until it fills my ears. The bowl is almost vibrating in my hands until finally, I blink. When I open my eyes, I am beneath the waves, everything below the water alive with light.

The path to Palm is lined with schools of specterfish and shoals of squid, the harmony of water rising through bridges and cities of coral. Everything beneath the waves has a sound, and for the first time I can hear all of it, see all of it. No wonder Mooneye never looks up from this thing. The *Moony* churns through the water below us, a thudding percussion over the waves that sends fish scattering in all directions.

Very good. Press your mind farther out into the waters.

Mooneye's voice is dryly impressed, so I take a deep breath and quest my mind out farther, racing past the constellations of bright fish and the dulled points of ship wreckage lodged between rocks like teeth. A faster rhythm churns out ahead, the waters curving around the edge of another Heaven, Palm.

I can feel the pulse of Palm's harbor just past the ends of my fingers, like holding a hand over someone's chest. I can see the shadows of trade boats weaving through their water marketplace. Somewhere in all this chaos, there has to be someone who knows how to find Dirge. Somewhere in the noise, his hidden name is spoken.

Nausea thrums through me, and my gut roils as if a small storm cloud were trapped inside me. A dry heave forces itself up my throat as if I might vomit.

You feel it, too. Good. Mooneye's tone is sad.

My vision beneath the water wavers, and I fight to calm myself. I focus again on the water, and my mind slips down again into the vision in the bowl. I breathe and look around beneath the waves. The ocean is hazy blues and greens, sea glass illuminated by a candle except for one spot. Dull and gray, like a cloud of dirt. When I try to reach my mind farther, I hear the sound of teeth gnashing and something guttural. A roar. No, not a roar, thunder.

My eyes snap open to find Mooneye staring back at me, unblinking.

"What was that thing?" I gasp, only just now realizing how long I have been holding my breath.

Mooneye's face contorts, and his vision returns to the bowl. "I can see no more than you can. It's a dead space in the water. It moves slowly, but there is pain wherever it goes. I can hear a bit of what is going on nearby, the same as I felt on the day your father went mis—" Mooneye flinches slightly.

I hear the water slosh in the bowl as I focus my energy to slow the *Moony*. Out in the distance, I can see the white oak towers of Palm. My only lead.

Unless.

"Mooneye, is it possible that the dead space in the water has to do with how the Pointers stole my father?"

Mooneye shifts uncomfortably, and the water in the bowl nearly spills. "It is *possible* but . . ."

"But what?" I say a little snappier than I meant to.

"I don't remember feeling the dead space actually *near* the captain during his fall. It was leagues away."

"But they could have swum it over to him when they took him?" I ask insistently as I begin to hear the bells and clamor of Palm just beyond my sight.

"I suppose they could have. Everything from the fall is a bit of a blur." Mooneye taps a beat on the edge of the bowl. "But I have to say that I don't love the idea of sailing into a situation not knowing what is waiting."

I bite my lip, thinking as the *Moony* groans to a crawl. Then, slowly at first, the bow of the ship turns away from Palm, heading north toward the sickly, dead-feeling water leagues ahead of us.

"Mooneye, send word below that there's been a change of plans." My voice is distant, resonant with magic, as the *Moony* gains speed, heading toward the unnatural quiet in the middle of the sea.

"Are we sure this is wise?" Mooneye says, already fishing the signal flare from the little pouch at his waist.

"Whatever that thing is, I feel in my bones the Pointers are involved. There could be Passengers in that water," I say, arms crossed and feeling the Mark of the Scythe warm as the magic of the *Moony* harmonizes with it and power floods through every inch of me.

"No matter what, we need to be there to help."

Mooneye nods dutifully and throws the bright blue flare in the air that signals Passengers on the water.

"Also throw the flare for top speed; everyone is going to want to hold on tight." I urge the *Moony* on faster, carrying us in a blur to the place where the water has died.

The diseased yellow-green glow of the Children of the Shark's ships cast the water in long shadows. Their skiffs circle a ship of Passengers, probably bound for a new life in Root. Above our heads, there's a suffocating number of storm clouds, which can only mean one thing.

"The *Stormblade*'s here, too." I groan, then find a smile at the edge of my lips.

Shard's Reaper ship is here. Shard, home of the only person in the Five Heavens that can bring the *Moony* down into the Depths. I never thought I'd be so happy to see those dyeheads!

My joy doesn't last long, though, as a clap of thunder swallows every other sound on the water, and the eerie green tides begin to churn faster from the center. Water slaps onto the starboard deck. I feel the tide yank at my core as I fight to keep the *Moony* from capsizing. Now's about the time that Dad would begin barking orders.

Well, like father, like daughter?

I grab one of the lines of rope docked to the crow's nest and salute Mooneye before diving off the side.

One perk of being captain? Sometimes Windthreader magic doesn't even need to be spoken, only felt in time with the ship. I somersault onto the deck near Sunshower, who is back-to-back with Gourd, fending off the approaching horde of Pointers, their near-translucent black teeth almost glowing in their pearl-white mouths. I hurl one of my knives into the chest of an advancing Pointer before spinning into formation with my back to Gourd and Sunshower.

"Well, look who graced us with her presence." Gourd grunts, sending a burst of wind toward a Pointer, who goes spinning backward into the grappling chain they had used to board the *Moony*.

I plant my feet and send a second gust that blows the enemy over the side of the ship with a satisfying splash.

"Captain always makes it a fair fight!" I grin, spinning up the Thousand Knives spell that turns the wind to blades that arc above my head.

"Everyone, duck!" I cry as I will the wind-knives to spin in a halo above me.

The ten surrounding Pointers hold themselves at bay, one glaring and snarling at the tattoo shining on my forearm.

I flick my wrist, and each of the wind-blades buries itself in a shark-demon's chest. Steam bursts from their chests, and they fall as the rain whips away the scent of rusted metal.

"Sunshower," I call as I wheel around to face him and Gourd, both their faces already shining with sweat. "Status report."

"Well," Sunshower begins, "we've been boarded."

"This is no time for jokes!" Gourd and I say in unison, then stare at each other, both impressed and surprised.

"No sense of humor," Sunshower mutters under his breath. "The *Stormblade* appears to have saved many of the Passengers from the . . ." Sunshower peers out with his Archer's eyes to the smaller ship, the kind of commercial schooner that brings food and supplies and relocates Passengers among the Five Heavens. It's still being circled by a skiff of Pointers menacingly swinging a long rusted chain. "*Rosebringer*," he finishes. "We need to bring the *Moony* level so the Ropers can get close enough to land and sweep the *Rosebringer* for Passengers before the Pointers get to them."

I sink deep into a stance like Dad's and let my mind slip toward only the navigation of the *Moony*. The stormy waves batter me from either side as I grit my teeth until it feels like they may shatter.

"Violet, you need to be calm to—" Gourd interrupts, but I put up a hand as I feel the ship beginning to turn.

The wood of the deck groans in protest, but the *Moony* surges forward. I crack open an eye and begin giving orders as the ship pulls level with the *Stormblade*.

"Sunshower, I need you to hit the prow of the *Rosebringer* on my mark."

"Can do!" Sunshower claps, already nocking an arrow to his bowstring.

"Gourd, you're going to give me a wind boost."

"A boost to where?!" Gourd shouts back, half her sentence lost in the crack of lightning.

I point to the *Rosebringer*.

Gourd's eyes widen before she shakes her head. "Absolutely not. It would be totally irresponsible for the captain of this ship to abandon her post and board another vessel! Your father never would!"

Ignoring Gourd's words, I gesture at Sunshower to loose his arrow to signal the crew to prepare for battle. Then on a rush of my own wind and Windthreader magic, I boost myself toward the *Rosebringer* to save who I can.

— 16 —

Pain leaps up my leg as I land off-balance on the deck of the *Rosebringer*.

A curse on every dye-headed Shard Reaper responsible for this storm.

I knuckle the rain from my eyes to see the situation aboard. Most of the deck is abandoned but for a few stray weapons and the chains of disused grappling hooks.

CRASH.

A massive sound comes from the rear of the ship, a snapping noise as if the *Rosebringer* is being pulled apart. The clamor of blades is almost swallowed by the sound of thunder above us. The deck bucks below me as I whirl and sprint toward the noise. Tonight, beneath the storm clouds, the tides are an endless mouth prepared to swallow the poor little ship whole.

When I arrive at the quarterdeck, a terrified Passenger no older than Moss scrambles backward on all fours from an advancing Pointer. The boy's mouth is wide with terror; the Pointer's mouth is wide with decaying fangs as it looms over the boy. The deck bucks again, briefly shooting the *Rosebringer* in the air before crashing down. The boy's willowy chest heaves with anxiety as he rolls to avoid a claw trying to pin him down. He looks left and right for someone to rescue him.

Me.

"Ayo, fang-brain!" I holler. The Pointer looks up with a confused expression and milky eyes. "I'm gonna—"

Before I have a chance to roast the ghost-shark, it's struck from above, a blue feathered bolt now sticking out of its chest. A second later, it melts into smoke and the bolt clatters to the ground.

Now it's my turn to look around, confused. A shadow drops to the deck gracefully, ruddy armor gleaming briefly in the light before they kneel to pick up the bolt.

I hurry over to the boy, offer him my hand and pull him to his feet, one eye on the shadowy figure.

"What's your name?" I ask the boy, checking him for wounds.

"Kai." The quiver of the boy's voice makes the one syllable vibrate.

"Kai with the beautiful name, I need you to stand behind me."

"That won't be necessary." The shadow's voice is high and clear, breaking through another crack of thunder. They almost sound *bored*.

They point, their finger nearly translucent as the lightning briefly illuminates their features. Their cheekbones sit imperiously high on their face, casting long shadows down their bearded face. A silky white scar curves along the outer edge of their left eye. They sweep a twilight-colored braid from their face and stare arrogantly down at me. On their opposite arm is a device, like a tiny bow into which another bolt has already been loaded.

"You, boy, have a chance to hop aboard the *Stormblade*." They stick out their palm, expectant. "I'd suggest you take it."

"I was about to take him to Horizon," I say, clearing my throat. "I'm Violet Moon, captain of the *Moony*."

The Shard Reaper shakes their head as they stare at me, blinking like they've only just remembered I was there.

"I believe the boy can make his own decision." They look past me again to Kai. "I'd imagine your mother would miss you, no?"

His mother must be one of the other Passengers the Shard Reapers have already saved and welcomed on their ship.

Kai steps out from behind me, nodding tremulously. The Shard Reaper smiles and offers their hand again, which Kai takes. He looks back at me with a guilty expression.

"The Shard Reapers have secured most of the remaining Passengers on this ship." The Reaper stares at me, comprehension dawning on their face. "Captain! Oh, you're the daughter of Virgil!"

Hearing Dad's name is like a fist to my gut.

"What are you doing here?" The Reaper looks at me quizzically as Kai's eyes boomerang between us.

I take a step forward, eyes narrowing. "I'm doing what Reapers have always done, same as you. And you are?"

"Branch. Branch Stormblade." They flick another twilight braid from their face as the rain intensifies. "And I meant, don't you need to be on board your own ship in order to—"

CRASH.

An enormous wave crashes down onto the deck as the sound of splintering wood fills my ears and water fills my boots. The waves are coming quick and fast now, the churn threatening to capsize the boat.

"Can you tell your buddies to turn it down, Branch Stormblade?!" I roll my eyes and begin to advance on them.

"The storm can only be directed, never tamed." Branch waves me off, beginning to walk back toward the aft portion of the ship, never stumbling even as the deck churns beneath us.

"You see, now you're saying that like it's gospel, but that just sounds like a poetic way of saying y'all don't know how to *aim!*" I call after Branch.

I hustle a step and a half to keep pace with them, Kai staring nervously up at the storm between the two of us, the clouds coiling over each other like ebony pythons.

"And anyway, I came down here because I wanted to see if you needed any assistance," I add.

Branch scoffs, the rain outlining them hazily.

"Didn't need your assistance before the *Moony* arrived; certainly do not need it now. You are relieved, Captain."

Rage flowers in my chest as I push my sleeves up over my elbows. *Who do they think they are?* I take a deep breath and try to calm down, the Mark of the Scythe glowing on my forearm.

A captain demands respect, Dad's voice says in my head. *They address things diplomatically. They represent their ship in all issues with peace and respect for—*

"Who do you think you're talking to?! Apologize before I toss you in the tide," I shoot back with a scowl.

All. Peace and respect for all.

Branch opens their mouth, but the sound of the ocean swallows their voice. It's not the pitch and keel of the waves lapping at the *Rosebringer*. Not the lightning fracturing the Heavens. Not the wet slap of the rain. The sound is a rotten deep note. It starts as a vibration in the marrow of my bones and rattles through my body like a piercing pain at the hinge of my jaw. Nausea sweeps through me, and alarm is etched in every line of Branch's weathered face.

Wordlessly, we rush to the side of the ship, the force of the sound splintering the wood of the railing. The eerie glow of the Children of the Shark's ships is bleeding away from beneath the *Rosebringer*. Instead, the mucus-yellow light is migrating, a stank moon, just to the edge of where the *Stormblade* and the *Moony* orbit the ship we're on.

And then, above the Children of the Shark's glow, the

tides begin to part. The awful sound swells like a hive. In my bones, I can feel that the dead place in the water is coming to the surface. The whirlpools churn as the hole eclipses the yellow water. Tonight, the tides are like an endless mouth swallowing ships and enemies alike. When five muscled Pointers emerge from the waves with an ornate stone jar as tall as Gourd between them, I learn there are things even an ocean can choke on.

— ✦ 17 ✦ —

"We need to regroup. NOW!" Branch's voice is brittle with horror as they snatch Kai's arm and begin to turn away from the oncoming Pointers and their mysterious, enormous jar.

I squint across the surf and see the five Children of the Shark nudge the jar gingerly to the edge of their skiff and tip its contents into the water.

There's no way, I mutter. *There's no such thing as a Slavetide.*

But the gray liquid that sluggishly plops out of the jar disagrees. Within its poisoned waters, tortured faces press to the surface only to be subsumed back into the filthy liquid seconds later. There is such a thing as a Slavetide, such a thing as cursed water that binds the souls of the Chainmakers. Nausea roils through me as I look at their distended mouths and furious eyes. This is the fate of the ones who built the ships, who chained the Sun People on the land from which we came.

Cursed to either be Pointers, or this. There is such a thing as water that cannot know mercy or peace, whose filth eats everything that it comes across like a school of wolffish and never stops coming.

The legends of the Slavetide are true.

And it is headed right for us.

I wheel and burst forward to run neck and neck with Branch as the moan of the Slavetide quiets the thunder above our heads.

"Hey, wait, I have a question for you," I say.

"Oh?" Branch huffs, pressing themself harder forward. "Does it start with a 'How do' and end with 'we escape'?"

"Well, no but—"

"Oh cool, then I recommend you direct that question to anyone except me!"

This is what happens when you give a whole people the power to make storms. I huff, head down against the rain. *A whole Heaven of Reapers in bad moods.*

"Look," Branch continues, "I need to regroup with the rest of our Ropers and help get everyone off to the *Stormblade* before the Slavetide swallows this ship. Are you totally useless with a blade?"

I snort and flick my knife from my belt into my other hand with a little flourish.

"Okay, great, a nonverbal answer to my time-sensitive question!"

I can almost hear Branch rolling their eyes. I grit my teeth as another wave of nausea rolls through and the Slavetide grows closer with a horrifying moan.

"Well, if you're anything like your father, you'll at least be a little help, because we've got company," Branch finishes, loosing a bolt that finds its home near the back fin of a Child of the Shark.

Branch is correct—an entire platoon of the shark-faced demons is crawling over the rails of the *Rosebringer* as a band of *Stormblade* Reapers dressed in maroon armor fends off the advancing swarm with arrows and long blades.

Branch kneels briefly at Kai's side. "Young one, I need you to go hide near . . ." Their moonlit eyes survey the nightmare landscape as a bone-chilling cracking noise shudders through the ship.

The deck of the *Rosebringer* tips to one side, and I put my palm to Kai's back as he stumbles near the edge of the ship.

"The Slavetide must be eating the boat!" I shout.

"Just go hide." Branch claps Kai on the shoulder, nearly knocking the little Passenger sideways.

Branch straightens and clicks their head in the direction of their battling crew, the Passengers cowering behind them as they fight valiantly against the chain-swinging demons.

"You take what I don't kill first." Branch can't resist a grin.

I return it with one of my own. "Nah, you take the right, I'll take the left."

Branch's eyes pop as they pass over the tattoo on my

forearm, like they didn't believe me earlier when I said I was captain. I smirk.

Finally, a captain's respect. I charge into the fray, leaping onto the back of a Pointer and driving my knife into the demon's chest before hopping backward onto the deck. My stomach rolls as I spin to my right, where a Pointer has noticed that they have me and Branch fighting them from opposite sides. I jab it in the gut, hook my leg behind it, and bring it crashing to the ground.

A few of the Shard Reapers have noticed my arrival, and I can hear the squeals of several more ghost-sharks falling as Branch advances slowly toward the crowd. It's been a long time since I saw the Reapers of Shard fighting up close. I have forgotten how much, to them, this is also a kind of dance.

At first, Branch is almost perfectly still, but when a Pointer swipes a broad claw, they duck before I can blink, and they pull the creature almost nose to nose with them before firing a bolt into its chest. The Pointer melts before it's even finished spinning to the ground. Branch snags the bolt out of the air and wields it like a knife, jabbing another enemy twice before loading that bolt into the small bow on their wrist and loosing it with lethal accuracy at a third.

Branch spins away from a fourth pursuer and yells something at me, but their voice is lost in the tumult as the *Rosebringer* sinks deeper into the water. I go to the railing only to see the Slavetide bubbling below the entire ship. The graying water is full of eyes and fingertips, not even water anymore but a violently clawing mass of endless bodies.

This is how the gods of the old world and the new cursed the Chainmakers for their hunger. I shake my head, nausea climbing through my bones at the sight. *Their regret eats everything, and yet they know no nourishment; they are fast and vicious, but they can never escape what they have made themselves into.*

"Reaper, orders?" asks a bold-looking Shard Reaper with a pair of long black tattoos ringing her scalp. She faces Branch as she wrenches one of her small spears from the last of the advancing horde of Children of the Shark.

Branch is all business, rigid and drawn to their full height in the light. "Reapers, the priority is to destroy the Slavetide and secure the safety of the rescued Passengers."

A murmur skips through the ranks of the Reapers behind me. The *Rosebringer* crunches and sinks some more.

"And the girl, Reaper?" says another Shard Reaper, a willowy Passenger whose armor sags around him.

"The girl," I interject, putting some bass in my voice to compete with the storm, "is Violet Moon, captain of the *Moony*. Also, KAI!" I holler out.

Kai pokes his head out from the inside of a barrel, his shadowy cheeks splitting into a smile as he runs across the deck and into the arms of a Passenger woman in a long, elegant dress the color of ash.

Branch stares a long moment at the two before resuming their orders. "Seed?"

The bald Reaper woman steps forward, a grim line in her jaw.

"You, Iniko, and Ashia need to guide the lightning to strike the Slavetide. Anything else will only be consumed or harmed by it."

"A second storm atop this one?" Seed clicks her tongue.

"It will require concentration, a lot of concentration," says the Reaper named Ashia.

"And protection," says the willowy Passenger Reaper, Iniko.

"You will have protection, Reapers," Branch replies reassuringly.

"From whom, Reaper? The wind?" Iniko shoots back. "You will be busy protecting the Passengers, and Chinara has already been taken."

None of the Shard Reapers flinch, though Branch's brow furrows. A new pang of nausea, different than the one caused by the Slavetide, hits my gut. The Reapers of the *Stormblade* have lost one of their own. A Reaper like me, like Dad. The cold of the rain melts away from my skin as lightning flares again, and I see his face pulled beneath the waves to the place of Slavetides and ghost-sharks, to a hell no one has the courage to seek out. Rage warms my hands, my throat, prickles in needles below my skin.

I step forward, a blade glimmering in each hand like the Mark of the Scythe beneath my sleeve. "I will protect the Stormcallers. We will wipe that abomination from the face of the sea."

⊷ 18 ⊶

Sixty, maybe even a hundred, tortured faces churn in the muck of the Slavetide below the decks of the sinking *Rosebringer*. Lightning illuminates the Shard Reapers as they hold hands and meet each other's eyes, and the air begins to hum around them. Blood pounds in my ears as I try not to look at the faces trapped in the Slavetide, the oily green glow of their eyes haunting me even when I blink.

"The Pointers will sense the storm building," Branch yells over the rising winds. "They will be drawn to it like lantern fish to . . ."

Branch Stormblade taps their chin before I offer, "Lanterns?"

"No," they muse as the tooth of the first grappling hook punches into the wood on the opposite side of the deck. "Something else. Something better," they drawl, casually shooting a bolt into the first Pointer's ugly jaw full of fangs.

I roll my eyes and stifle a groan as the chant of the Storm-callers behind me drones louder and faster.

"Ashes to ashes, dust to the Chainmakers. Ashes to ashes, dust to the Chainmakers."

The crew drones on, and I open my mouth to speak to my own winds, to thread them into a story, into a thousand knives that spin and flourish before me like the petals of a fire rose. A crunch echoes through the ship as it continues to sink into the swirling maw of the Slavetide.

"Just my luck, the rumors of Slavetide sickness are true." I growl, gritting my teeth in an attempt to ignore my roiling gut and focus.

I look over my shoulder to see a dark cloud forming between the Stormcallers, floating into the sky and drinking in the rain. It coils and expands like a serpent until the storm cloud flashes with lightning and multiplies. The first bolt of lightning strikes the water and a wet scream splashes up from the souls trapped in the Slavetide.

Branch can't suppress a grin and fires a bolt with white feathers into the sky. It whistles a high, unmistakable sound before exploding with blue light and disappearing.

The nearby *Stormblade* banks to the left, approaching the prow of the *Rosebringer*, and its crew tosses five ropes in our direction.

For a massive ship, I think, annoyed at how impressed I am, *the* Stormblade *can turn in a heartbeat.*

Branch and two other Shard Reapers catch the ropes in

hand, and Branch fires a bolt into the ground to anchor the ropes. Meanwhile, I hear a second grappling hook and a third punch into the wood near the trio of Stormcallers who are now in a shouting match with the storm, the lightning multiplying like a wave of arrows.

How did I get stuck defending the Stormcallers? I think as a clawed fin hauls a stinking demon over the side of the ship. The creature swipes a leg out at me, but I backflip and dodge it by seconds before launching a wind-knife into its shoulder. The Pointer gives a wet scream that is followed by a sick crunch as I rocket forward and punch it full in the face.

Oh right. I volunteered. I grin and shove the creature over the railing.

"Wind, old friend, friend who sings a hundred names," I begin, drawing my hands before me in a circular motion and feeling the air tremble. "Be my wall, be the hands where I cannot."

The winds roar their answer and form a bulb of vicious air around me and the Stormcallers, forming a barrier between us and the Pointers.

But the wind barrier can't protect us from the destruction of the oncoming Slavetide. I hear more sounds of splitting wood as the ship is devoured further. For a moment, the thunder is more of a hiccup in the wind as the Stormcallers' chants falter.

In that brief space of time, a Pointer's fist slams into my chest. Pain sears my rib as the world snaps into focus and I find myself driven back-to-back with the Stormcaller named Iniko, now nearly pulled to her knees by the growing nausea. The Pointer that caught me off guard brings both arms down like hammers. I barely roll to avoid the blows, but the move sets my stomach off, bubbling with acid and churning just like the Slavetide below, the spoiled smell leaking into the air.

I swallow hard to keep the bile down. Now more Pointers are finding their footing and advancing against the slowing storm. Behind me, the shark-demon answers a garbled roar from its brothers and pivots away from me to the Stormcallers. And there's Iniko, teeth gritted, forcing herself back upright against the nausea and the endless moan of the Slavetide. I risk a glance down at the tide and see it's swallowed half the ship now.

We're sinking. I'm helpless. We're sinking. I'm helpless. My mind races as I try to force myself upright. *I'm going to die before I make it to Dad. It's all my fault, again.*

Despair takes me by the throat as I see the gleaming jaws of the Pointers, almost grinning with savage hunger. The Pointer that busted my rib raises a claw to strike at the Stormcallers, and I feel rage flood my veins. I spot an abandoned grappling chain next to me on the side of the ship and summon the wind to me. I bellow, and the chain is ripped out of the wooden railing and slams into the head of the attacking Pointer. It screams in agony and rage as it wheels and charges at me. Another pang of Slavetide-induced nausea rattles through my bones. But my anger pulls me up straighter, teeth gritted so hard they may crack. But not before I let loose another howl and charge, eyes darting between the beast and the chain behind it.

The wind moves immediately at my thought. Buffeting winds surge around the Stormcallers blowing away several of the invading Pointers. The grappling chain slithers around the Pointer's ankle, tripping it. I plunge my knife where its heart once was. Triumph washes over me, and all the anger in my body burns the nausea away. I will not die helpless; I'm Virgil and Pearl Moon's daughter. I'm Captain Violet Moon, and I'm not losing anyone else.

I scowl and beckon the slippery beasts forward.

The leader, a black-fanged hammerhead demon, howls as three Pointers charge forward and melt on contact with the swirling wind shield.

"Oh, did I forget to mention that was sharp?" I feel a rush of power needle through my veins, the Mark of the Scythe glowing so brightly I can almost see it through the sleeve of my jacket.

The milky eyes of the Pointer grow dark with alarm. Meanwhile, the Slavetide groans as more lightning strikes down on it, a hundred threads of the brightest storm I have ever seen. I survey the deck as Branch ushers the last of the Passengers from the *Rosebringer* across the ropes toward the *Stormblade* with one hand and fends off their own boarding party on the port side of the ship. I turn my eyes back to the hammerhead leader, who is looking up and back between the still chanting Stormcallers and me, my other knife still in hand.

"By the way," I say, I guess to nobody because the Stormcallers can't hear me and Pointers never speak, "so long as you're looking up . . ."

I point and watch the demon's eyes follow my finger as the wind-blades lying in wait above its head rain down on the Child of the Shark, melting it.

I smirk, the magic of the *Moony* flowing through my veins. I am the captain I have always meant to be; I am the Reaper I always dreamed of being. I'm Violet, daughter of Virgil and the most powerful I have ever—

BOOM!

An explosion rocks the decks, rainwater sloshing in all directions. I whip my head around to see a grim expression on Branch's face, arm extended as a single bolt from the bow on their arm appears to have liquified at least five Children of the Shark. My jaw hangs open. Branch turns and winks before saluting and preparing to mount the ropes.

"What did you . . . ? How did you . . . ? Could you do that the whole time?!" I yell over the biting winds.

"Yes. Now, please return my Reapers once you're done cleaning up this mess." Branch gestures at the ocean, the screeches of the Slavetide fading.

I'm about to respond when I feel a gut-bending pain radiate through me. In my forearm, beneath the Mark of the Scythe, it feels like bone scraping against bone.

The concerns of the Stormcallers are muffled as my throat grows tight. The scene begins to swim before my eyes. I'm driven to my knees and shrug off the concerned hand of one of the Stormcallers.

My eyes scan around, desperate for an answer. I roll up my sleeve and for the first time since Dad fell, since I became captain of the *Moony*, I see the light of the Mark of the Scythe flicker.

CRUNCH-BOOM-CRACK.

The three sounds come in quick succession as I force myself to my feet and stumble to the railing to vomit into the roiling dark waters. I wipe the rain from my eyes and look at the *Moony*.

My father's ship, my ship, has a massive hole in the side as the last of the Slavetide drains from it. I feel as if I will be sick again, rage and despair coming in waves as I gasp for air. I wanted to do what Reapers do, to save Passengers. But instead I did what a captain should never do. I abandoned my ship when she needed me most.

A growl forces its way out of my throat and becomes a bellow, a scream. The storm takes notice. A single streak of lightning follows my fury and obliterates the last of the Slavetide with a guttural moan that shakes the waves.

I don't remember what I say as the Ropers of the *Moony* land on the decks of the sinking *Rosebringer* and pull me onto my damaged, barely floating ship. My ignored family all look to me, and their eyes are heavy.

Gourd's mouth is a thin line, her eyes scoured red. Moss kicks at invisible dust with his feet. The Ropers untie their lines from their belts. The storm fades from the sky and moonlight beams across the rain-soaked deck. Everyone is here; everyone is disappointed.

Everyone, except Sunshower.

I see Mooneye and sink to my knees again. Mooneye's not in the crow's nest, where he should be, looking down at his ornate bowl. It lies at his side, dented and emptied of water. And he has no brother at his side to comfort him. I peer at the crew. Wordlessly, they shake their heads and look below to the churning tides. I know without needing to be told aloud that Sunshower was abducted, just like Dad.

A surge of wind builds around me as a scream rips out of my throat. I am the captain of a sinking ship, I am the Reaper who failed her crew, I am the most powerful I have ever been—and I am powerless to stop us from losing Sunshower for good.

— 19 —

Maybe Gourd thinks that I can't feel what is happening to the ship while I wait, confined to the captain's quarters, as she negotiates with the Reapers of the *Stormblade* about how to resolve my mistake.

Mistakes, plural, I remind myself with a huff.

The room isn't helping of course. I've been coming to this room since I first toddled in on sea legs, Dad behind the desk attending to one thing or another. He made it all look so easy.

I wander around the room as dusty light wavers from the candle. I drag my finger along the desk and smile despite myself. Sometimes Dad's arms would be moving so fast the Mark of the Scythe would blur with the speed, and I would dream of the day it would fit me.

Now, I glare at the tattoo, still dimly flickering. It gives off a low thudding pain like a bruise as I feel the wood of the *Stormblade* being fused to our hull.

One voyage as a captain, and I'll be lucky if I end up grounded back on Horizon forever.

I cock my head as I hear the hinges of the door whine. Gourd steps in.

I draw myself to my full height and meet Gourd's eye. But she won't look at me. She sweeps past and sits at the table still covered in maps and gestures at the empty seat in front of her. I sit, waiting and watching the pale drops of wax roll down the length of the candle.

Gourd finally punctures the silence, the words coming off her tongue slowly. "The Reapers of the *Stormblade* say that you fought valiantly. They will tow us as far as the shores of Root and then need to return to Shard with the Passengers that I am told you"—Gourd's eyes flash up and meet mine— "were instrumental in saving."

I straighten in my seat, trying not to look relieved or confused. I expected Gourd to blow up at me, to scream, to chastise, to punish.

"You did an honorable thing. Passengers are free from the enemy's clutches because of what you did. The Reaper Iniko was . . . especially insistent I note that to you."

Then Gourd's brow furrows, creasing the clean lines of her fade at her temples. My stomach turns to stone as my mouth twists like a snake.

"However, the praise stops there." Gourd sighs. "Do you know how many languages are spoken in the Five Heavens?"

I cock an eyebrow. "Eighteen? Twenty-eight? Thirty-eight? More?" I muse.

"The answer is that I don't know." Gourd taps the desk with her knuckle.

"What?"

"I have no idea how many languages are spoken on the Tides of the Lost because I have not been everywhere, nor do I know everything. For all I know, there are hundreds of languages, perhaps sixty million and more. But I wouldn't know, because I do not know everything. I do not *presume* to know everything. And I am many years your elder."

My breath catches in my chest. Gourd is rarely truly angry. People mistake her volume for her anger. But when truly furious, she gets quiet. With each word, Gourd's voice is drawing nearer to a hush.

"Gourd, I—"

But Gourd stops me with a hand. "*I do not know everything* is also something Sunshower says—used to say."

I flinch at the mention of his name, the memory of his golden smile twisting my insides.

Gourd taps the table sharply with her knuckles for attention. "Sunshower encouraged me to leave you be after Virgil died. To let you process however you needed to process. To not advocate that the captaincy be passed to someone with more experience. To gift you space."

My shoulders slouch and feel like they will not stop until

they slide off my body all together. Gourd's voice is sharp and low now, building in speed.

"He told me that you are the only person who knows the fullness of how you are feeling. Who knows what kind of leader you will be." Gourd pinches the bridge of her nose. "The only person, according to Sunshower, who knows everything about what you're feeling is you. And, aside from maybe Moss"— Gourd's eyes roll—"You are also the only one who knows what you have been planning for the last couple days."

All the hair on my arms leaps to attention as alarm springs through my chest.

It must show on my face because Gourd's frown deepens, and she nods stiffly. "So, Violet, would you please do me the courtesy, now that Sunshower has paid for it with his life, of telling me what exactly it is you've been planning?"

I wince again, picturing Sunshower like Dad. Sunshower in the water, the waves pulling him closer and closer until the lightning flashes.

A long sigh escapes me, and I feel my whole body deflate. "There's a super-soldier from Shard by the name of Dirge . . ." I begin, spreading my hands over the maps as I tell Gourd the full story of everything Moss and I have been up to.

At the end, Gourd glowers at me.

"So, now I'm certain of a couple things. One: You are your father's daughter. And two: You are not yet prepared to be the Reaper he was."

Color drains from my face, but Gourd's eyes are unblinking as she continues.

"Violet, no matter how many languages are spoken on the Tides of the Lost, I am certain there are no words for how disappointed Virgil would be to know that you abandoned your post when you were needed most. Do you think it didn't anguish him not to be in the waters saving Passengers?"

Dad's face gulped down by the waters flashes behind my eyes. I flinch, and shame blooms beneath my cheeks.

Gourd's voice softens, just a little, as she continues, "It hurt him to be the protected one, to be the one everyone turned to with their problems. But he recognized he had just two hands, two legs, one mind. His capacity was not limitless. And he recognized, deep in his bones, that he had only one ship, one thing to protect above all others because it was what his community needed. What his crew needed, because without him the ship could not steer, could not move but for the whims of the breeze and the Windthreaders.

"He never abandoned his post because that is what a crew is for. A captain delegates, a captain prioritizes, a captain knows where their duties lie. And that is why from the moment he became captain and that"—Gourd jabs an elegant finger at the Mark of the Scythe—"icon was on his arm, he never left his post until the day it killed him."

"He's not dead," I mutter, my voice bouncing off the polished wood walls.

"Excuse me?" Gourd meets my eyes, and I can see the edges of hers are still red from lack of sleep, or maybe crying.

"He's not dead," I say again flatly.

"You don't know that," Gourd responds.

"Neither do you." Anger and despair lace my voice. "You don't know that he's dead. You didn't see him fall. You didn't see him dragged beneath the—You don't know that he's dead. None of you do." I pound my fist against the table, the candle rattling in its silver holder.

"Violet," Gourd attempts, but my voice is building and taller than me now.

"You and the council and the whole Heaven. Everyone was so eager to see him gone, and I'm the only one who's lifted a finger to save him. I'm the only who has done anything. The only one who misses him."

Tears prick the edge of my vision, and the captain's quarters fracture like a mirror as I fight to keep down the sob burrowing in my chest.

Gourd's fist slams the table so hard the candle nearly topples to the ground as the shadows in the room sway. "I can miss him. I *do* miss him." Gourd's shuddering breaths rasp between words. "I can miss Virgil and still be mad at him. Still boil at the thought that my closest friend in the world left without a word. I can be livid that he left his lone responsibility to a child." Gourd looks at me, the bags beneath her eyes swollen.

"A brave child, but a child. And then he left that child with me. I can miss him and still be mad at him. I'm doing it right now, as I speak to you, as I bargain with Shard to tow us to my old home. I can miss him and still do my job. Can you say the same?"

Some of the rage flows out of my shoulders, and I feel like I could sleep for three days. Gourd looks at me, sympathy in her eyes for a moment before they harden.

She continues, "The burden he left you with is too great. We will stay the next few nights with my cousin, Rain, in Root. We will manage repairs, and then we will sail back to Horizon, where I will recommend that the council force you to pass the command of the *Moony* to me until you reach seventeen years."

The words ring around me as I feel the *Stormblade* begin tugging us forward to Root. Five years off the ship? Five years from being able to rescue Dad and Sunshower? Five years, alone?

"Gourd, I—"

But Gourd rises imperiously and makes her way to the door.

"The decision is final. You should get some rest."

As I step out onto the deck, the moon shines clean along the ship's wooden planks. I do not feel like resting. I do not feel like if I close my eyes, I will see anything but Dad's and Sunshower's faces crushed beneath the waves. I look at the moon, a wavering crescent framed by clouds as Moss steps to my side.

"Were you listening to that whole conversation?" I say, not looking down.

"I was." Moss pouts. "What are we gonna do now, Vi?"

"We, my friend," I muse, walking toward the bridge of enchanted wood that binds the *Moony* to the *Stormblade*, "are going to find a way to make all this worth it."

~ 20 ~

A dusty quiet clings to everything on the deck of the *Storm-blade* as Moss and I cross the bridge between the vessels.

"So we're just going to try to find the Shard Reaper you fought alongside before?" Moss pipes up once our boots are on deck.

"I don't see another choice, honestly. Plus, who better to know about a secret Shard Reaper than a Reaper from Shard. This will be way faster than heading to Palm," I say, trying to convince myself as much as Moss. I look at the Mark of the Scythe on my arm, dull in the moonlight. "I can't give up yet. This can't have all been for nothing."

Moss nods as we walk the deck of the other Reaper ship. The *Stormblade* is much vaster and taller than the *Moony*. Looking down from the top deck, I can feel the difference between the magics of the *Moony* and the *Stormblade*. Where the *Moony*'s magic moves in a quick, flighty rhythm, the sliver of a fish's fin as it disappears beneath the water, the *Stormblade* is the muffled slap of a wave. At the point of the prow, the *Stormblade* lives up to its name, filing to a spear's point, where the deck of the *Moony* rounds.

One rides the tide, the other stabs it, I think as I scan the deck for the entrance to the crew quarters and find only dark polished wood.

"You won't find it, y'know," comes a voice from above.

I startle, then scowl upward at Branch sitting on the cross point of a mast.

"The entrance is hidden to keep the fang-brains out." Branch drops to the deck with barely a sound and straightens to look me in the eye. "I presume this midnight visit is about more than insomnia?"

"How'd you know to wait for us?" Moss asked.

"Well, youngling"—Branch leans over the edge of the ship—"once you get to be my age, you just wait for what's supposed to come your way. You hear the moment when it's coming to you. Destiny's got a sound, just like anything else."

Branch's eyes are far away on a distant point in the horizon.

I bite my lip and flex the muscles in my legs to keep them from shaking. "Have you ever heard of a soldier named Dirge?"

A loose bark of a laugh pops out of Branch's mouth, and they toss their head back before letting out another.

"Hey!" I stamp my foot, impatient.

Branch trains their gaze on me, wrestling the amusement

out of their face before saying much more seriously, "My apologies, young Captain, you've been sent on a chase for a myth."

I feel hollowed out by the words, as if someone has plunged their hand into my chest and scooped out my heart, my lungs, my stomach and left just a shell to stare dumbfounded at Branch.

Branch bows their head apologetically. "Every few months or so, some new trainee ends up hearing this myth of a supersoldier who traveled aboard the *Stormblade* to the Depths. Or went on a mission with the Reapers of Crest out in the Fang Waves. Or rode a whale the size of the moon to personally serve Death his saltfish stew. And I've been around since nearly the beginning of Shard. It's how I ended up spearpoint of this ship."

"Spearpoint?" Moss asks, stroking his chin pensively.

"I believe that you *Moony* folks would call it a first mate?"

"Well, how long have you been spearpoint?" I ask, trying to squeeze the mounting worry out of my voice.

"It's been two hundred thirty-five years," Branch rattles off, eyes fixed back on the horizon where dim blue lights play across the sky. "Like I said, I have been here a long time. New recruits come and go; they shake their fists at the skies, the tide, the gods who gifted us this place and never undid its curses."

"I thought that was just how Shard Reapers are." I scowl as a quiet laugh shakes Branch's shoulders.

"You really are just like him," Branch says wistfully.

"Virgil was also skeptical of Reapers who love to fight, Shard Reapers especially."

I smile proudly at the idea of Dad roasting the Shard Reapers at every opportunity.

Branch studies my face, and behind their smile I can feel something tighten. "You are not so different from some of our recruits. It was too soon, even for Virgil, to leave you with a burden like this."

I bite my lip and wince when I taste the tang of my own blood in my mouth.

"I'm sorry, little Reaper, I really am. I wish I had better news for you . . ." Branch trails off as the blue lights of the horizon draw closer, the thin clouds glow with greens and pinks, and lines of light as purple as my name shift like layers of silk over one another.

I look at Moss and smile despite myself at his wide-eyed wonder over Root's sky.

"We will be arriving soon, maybe you should catch your friend up on the legend of the Star-Drenched Baobab. Always puts me right to sleep, thinking what people from Root consider a good story."

Moss giggles at that, and a sad grin plays across Branch's face.

"But it is a story, just like the myth of Dirge. You may as well be hunting the Mother of Teeth. If a muscle-bound man could have gone on a mission to the Depths, there would be no keeping secret the story of what she did. A soldier like that would be captain of this ship by now."

Dirge is just a story. The *Moony* has a huge hole in it. I'm about to lose the captaincy of a ship with a hole in it. Over a story. Over some words made up to make little kids feel better. To make me feel better.

In the distance, beneath the swaying Technicolor of the sky above Root, I can see the outline of Root's flagship, the *Sagewind*. At the top somewhere, I know there's a flag with the image of the Star-Drenched Baobab. Another story, another myth, but one you can see and touch and eat the fruits of. A legend only the Heaven with soil can believe in.

Not like Dirge, I think, ashamed as my heart craters into my gut.

What a fool I've been. I've lost Dad and Sunshower and any last drop of hope that remained.

— 21 —

You'd think an agrarian Heaven would be dull, all low greens and muted browns. But the lights of Root glimmer in long silk wraps of azure and coral as Moss and I sneak back aboard the *Moony*. We stand at the prow as night melts into day and the low thatched huts of the Heaven of Root sprawl below us, lit in brilliant purple by the Star-Drenched Baobab. Above every small farm and port, Windthreaders call on the wind to shake rice from its stalks into huge sacks held open by the hands of the living and Passengers alike. The massive tree stretches into the sky, as if it means to scrape the bottom of the nearest constellation.

I nudge Moss in the ribs as he knuckles sleep from his eyes. "You trying to hear the story of how that tree got its colors?"

Moss tilts his head back, likely wondering if he's awake enough to make it to the end of the story. He nods, too tired to agree.

"Well, it's the most interesting story of a tree on the Tides of the Lost," I begin, guiding Moss back below deck where he can sleep a bit before we dock at the waiting harbor.

"Isn't it the *only* story of a tree on the Tides of the Lost?" Moss tries to cover his yawn as we descend the stairs.

"It is. But that makes it all the more special." I smile. "Long ago, the Chainbreakers of the *Sagewind* began their search for a new home. They prayed to the gods of the old world and the new, and the gods responded not with words, but with a light like a star on the surface of the ocean. And so the Chainbreakers sailed toward this star, and when they docked the ship they found an island with soil as rich and black as their own good hands, and then . . ."

I tap my chin, trying to remember what happens next. Luckily, Moss is helpful, especially when it comes to stories.

"And then they looked to the skies and asked the gods, right?"

I smile down at Moss, the gaps in his teeth like the skyline of Palm. I pull his head onto my shoulder, calmed by his familiar weight.

"That's right! The Chainbreakers looked to the skies and let the soil fall through their fingers and asked, *How can something grow in the absence of the sun? What kind of harvest can bloom from stars so dim?* In answer, the stars they could see dimmed for just a moment, and the soil of Root began to quake as the first thing to grow in the Tides of the Lost was a baobab tree that drank from the stars. The first Reapers of

Root became the farmers of all Five Heavens. They pulled the seeds of the old world from their braids and found that the Star-Drenched Baobab made light that their harvest could feast on."

I look at Moss, his light snoring a buzz at my shoulder.

"And so it was," comes a voice from nearby, startling me. Mooneye leans in the doorway. "That the people who came from the sun found themselves nourished by the light of different stars."

A pang goes through me to see Mooneye out of his normal perch. In the shadows of the flickering candlelight, he looks somehow even gaunter. All the parts of his face that are also Sunshower's face are almost impossibly sad and tired.

"Mooneye, I—" I move to get up, but Mooneye sidles up to sit alongside me.

"Violet, may I share something?" Mooneye's voice is soft, dry like an old scroll.

"Of course." My lips purse, prepared for another lecture I deserve on how I've ruined everything over a fairy tale.

"I miss Sunshower, dearly. It has torn something in me, to be able to see everywhere but where he is." Mooneye's breath rattles, a sob choking through him as Moss turns over in his sleep and curls into himself.

"Mooneye, I am so sorry. If I had been here, I—"

"Would have been as helpless as I have been for twenty-six years to stop my brother from choosing to defend the people he loves." Mooneye's shoulders still before he turns to make eye contact with me. "I'm not especially adept with feelings."

"Apparently, neither am I." I chew my lip.

"Well, that's two things we have in common." Mooneye chuckles. "Three if you count being prepared to tear down the sky if it means the return of my brother."

The words are quiet, but they still strike me in the face.

"I came because I want you to know that I do not blame you, *and* I wanted to know that I could come to you. The crew has lost its friend, its hero, but I have lost my brother as well. You were the first to know this kind of loss, and I hope we can be each other's guide and friend to the other side of it."

I pull Mooneye into a rib-cracking hug and nod. I hadn't thought of it before, but in some ways, he is the only one who knows what I am going through.

"All right, well, probably best for all of us to get some sleep . . . you included." Mooneye wags a finger at Moss's sleeping form. "Follow the little one's example. You'll need your rest. Gourd's cousin, Rain, is . . . a bit much."

When we arrive at Gourd's cousin's farm, I realize that Mooneye was right—Rain is really *something*. I mean, it is incredibly kind for her to take the crew up in her huge home and feed us some of the *best* jollof I've ever tasted. But, there is a problem.

Rain thinks she's *really* funny. And she's just . . . not.

The next morning's light pours through the window, and the house is filled with the sounds of chopping and . . . *It can't be.*

I roll quickly out of bed and throw on some nicer clothes before coming into the dining space to find Rain and Gourd chopping vegetables and laughing.

Who knew Gourd could laugh?!

"Ay, blessed morning, namesake!" Rain booms, pointing for the fourteenth time at the bright purple dye of her hair.

"Good morning." I cringe, trying for a that-joke-just-gets funnier-and-funnier grin.

Judging by Gourd's grimace, I can tell I did not succeed. It doesn't matter because Rain is doubled over with laughter, again.

"What were you laughing at before I arrived?" I ask, sitting on a stool.

"An old memory," Gourd answers, voice clipped as she resumes chopping okra.

"Of the days before Gourd-Gourd here left us and our fancy tree to go pursue the life of adventure she'd always wanted."

I stifle a snort at *Gourd-Gourd* but keep listening.

"Gourd wanted a life of adventure?" I ask, trying to imagine Gourd as a kid and drawing a blank .

"Well, of course she did. It's how she met your dad and—"

WHAM.

The knife Gourd had been chopping okra with trembles

on its edge as she slams it down. Silence reigns over the room as Rain looks between Gourd and me, wide brown eyes somehow growing wider.

"*O-kay* . . . Violet, would you grab that charming little Passenger and head to the central market? I could use some more wild onions for the stew tonight."

"Eager to!" I say as Gourd takes a steadying breath and yanks the knife out of the table to inspect it for dings.

We step outside, and Rain kneels to meet me at eye level.

"I've known my cousin for a long time. She didn't have the easiest time growing up here."

"Because she had to sit through your jokes?" Moss says at a volume he doesn't realize other people can hear.

"No, I'd bet that was the highlight!" She guffaws, slapping her thigh. "But in all seriousness, she's gonna come back around to you. But now it's maybe your turn to give *her* some space."

I grimace and nod dutifully.

"Now, you head off to the market and remember to go to the shop with the red awning, not the blue."

"Is there a reason?" Moss pokes his head up curiously.

"Yes, that man has never laughed at my jokes, and that's why his onions are only the size of your fist, not mine."

Moss and I make our way to the market, the bustle and the thick scent of fresh produce hanging in the air.

"So, are we giving up on finding Dirge?" Moss finally asks, all the words in one burst as if he's been holding them in for ages.

"I'm not sure." I sigh, pretending that I know where I'm going but really just staying behind a gang of gossiping teens carrying flasks of water and bags of uncooked rice. The four of them walk in a big line, which keeps us out of earshot of the rest of the crowd.

"But it feels like we have to, right?" I ask.

We arrive at the stand with the red awning, which is filled with plump onions. I pick a few and walk up to the stall owner.

"If we do that, then how would we complete the mission?"

"Maybe there is no mission anymore." I frown, handing the exact change to the man under the red awning.

He grins and loudly exults, "You must be Rain's new girl!"

The places a bad joke will get you recognized; I honestly don't think I'll ever understand it.

That night, I dream for the first time in days. Darkness surrounds me on all sides, silent except for a long, slow dripping sound. I feel my heart thud in my chest as if it is trying to escape. But escape to where, to what?

All I can see, all I can touch, is darkness. Until I reach my hand out and find another larger hand reaching to touch it. My gasp echoes as I step forward and feel the hand disappear. I step back, and the hand reappears. I step back and step back until I'm staring at my father, and while his mouth moves, there is no sound. Only him staring at me as I hear the dripping turn to the crackle of fire. I spin around and see nothing until I look at Dad again, surrounded by flames made of seawater.

I startle awake, drenched in sweat with moonlight spilling through the window. I quickly put on an outfit and slide my throwing knives into my boots. And because my mind is on Dad and my eyes are on the moon, I do not register the hooded figure drop down from the thatched roof behind me. I do not hear them creep up behind me. I hear nothing until the cock of the crossbow sounds.

The voice that comes is cold in the moonlight, like the point of the bolt at the back of my neck.

"I only wish to ask this once: Who are you? And what has brought you here, looking for Dirge?"

— 22 —

A bead of sweat rolls down my face as I consider the arrow's point at the back of my neck. I chance a glance behind me to try to clock whoever has gotten the drop on me. The head of the arrow pricks my skin as the mysterious voice repeats itself, echoing, tinny.

"Look, this doesn't have to be hard. You tell me where you heard that name and what you're doing here, and *maybe* I'll let you go." My attacker huffs.

I ball my hands into fists, crouch just a little.

"What was that name again?"

The attacker sighs in exasperation, relaxing their arm half an inch before saying again, "Last time. Who are you, and where did you hear about Dir—"

I lean forward hard and drive the heel of my boot into their midsection, a wheeze escaping my attacker. I wheel on the ball of my foot and sink into a fighting stance before I scan my opponent.

They are wiry and not much taller than me and are wearing a dark green hood over an inlaid iron mask with two horns emerging from the top and three shark's teeth forming a small goatee beneath the mouth. Behind the mask, only their gray eyes are visible, hard with fury as they fire the bolt off their wrist and charge.

I duck to avoid the bolt and spin left, throwing my arm up just in time to block a punch from the Iron Mask. I throw an uppercut of my own aimed for their gut, but they catch me by the wrist, pulling me close against their chest. I swing my leg behind theirs and shove hard.

Iron Mask stumbles back but doesn't fall, instead swinging an elbow into the side of my skull. I squeeze my eyes shut, willing the ringing out of my ears as I attempt to block an incoming punch but miss by inches. A split second later, a fist drives into my gut, launching me into the air before I crash to the ground. Storm clouds congeal over my head as the lightest drizzle rains down my face.

Another bolt whistles over me and lands near my head as my vision clears and I look at Iron Mask.

"I don't want to have to kill you."

"Don't worry." I grunt, springing up from the ground and summoning the Thousand Knives. "You won't."

Iron Mask makes a noise somewhere between a laugh and a groan before unclipping the hood around their shoulders. It drops with a heavy thud. Thunder roars as they charge. I send a vortex of wind-knives that they dodge with a series of flips that make them look like a leaf in the wind. Iron Mask backflips to my right, punches coming faster than I can blink, forcing me to retreat.

"You. Keep. Swinging. On. Me." I huff, sweat mixing with the rain and stinging my eyes.

"You will—" I grab their wrist and swing their momentum behind them.

"Draw back—" I grunt. The thunder bellows.

"A nub," I finish.

I spin the stunned attacker around and pull them into my knee, driving the breath from their lungs. Iron Mask turns their face up, and I swing my free fist into their ear and see the mask spin to the ground, one horn stabbed into the dirt.

Lightning cracks against the sky as the assassin? the guard? the bounty hunter? scowls at their iron mask, then at me. I snarl back, and we meet again in the middle, a complex dance of fists and legs until finally Iron Mask aims a crackling bolt at my chest, and I feel the Mark of the Scythe glow on my arm, and the light illuminates *her* face.

She looks about my age, has high cheekbones; a silver ring pierces her right nostril, and a crisp fade ends in a mohawk in the center of her black hair. One side of her head shows off an elaborate tattoo of a wing.

"The boy made of wings." I gasp, watching Iron Mask's eyes widen in alarm.

The bolt fires from the bow on her wrist, but not before I hit her there, messing up her aim. The bolt scream-whistles into the sky and shatters into a heavy rain as I shove her away. This time my foot behind her ankle does work, and I leap on top of Iron Mask, pinning her to the ground with my knife in my hand.

"Yield," I growl.

Iron Mask snarls in response, the wing tattoo at the side of her head now unmistakable in the light.

"You're not Fog." She spits.

"I'm not. I'm Annoyed and captain of the *Moony*. Now, you introduce yourself." I glare.

All the girl offers is stony silence.

"Okay, seriously. What is your problem?" I grimace. "I was just trying to get out of here. I've had a bad night of sleep and an even worse last few days. So who are you? His security? How did you learn Branch's signature move? What are you, like, Dirge's daughter or something?!" I shake the girl by her collar, and she shoves me off her but doesn't attack further as she sits up.

The clouds above begin to part as a great laugh rises from the main house of Gourd's cousin's farm; everyone must still be at the story night Rain was putting on.

"I'm sorry—" Iron Mask begins.

"Well, you should be," I answer, tending to a growing bruise on my chin.

"Not to you." She waves, rubbing at a similar bruise on her face. "What I was saying is that I'm sorry, did you say something about Branch's signature move?"

I shake my head in annoyance. "Yeah, the rain bolt or the lightning needle or . . ."

"Stormbolt," Iron Mask says drearily. "It's called the Stormbolt. Everyone always wants to make the names so complex, y'know? Just name the thing after the thing it does."

Iron Mask rocks herself up to her feet and takes on an imperious, formal tone like Gourd presenting in front of the council or talking about anything that lets her say the word *duty* a lot.

"Like, they call it the Grand Glass Lightning of Iron Mask of the Manacled Tide of the . . ."

"Elegant Storm's Endless Wing," I finish, mimicking the impression.

Iron Mask snorts with laughter and smacks her knee. "Yeah, see, you get it; by the time you say the whole name of the move—"

"You could have already punched them five times," I finish, the bruise on my chin throbbing as we both laugh.

"Six on a good day!" Iron Mask sighs as she kneels to pluck the mask from the ground, frowning at the mud, then glancing at me and the Mark of the Scythe.

"Okay, so I won't front; I think I *might* have been a lil too aggressive with my question. You're clearly not from Shard on some mission to prove yourself, and you're certainly not from here. So how does a child end up captain of one of the great Reaper ships?"

I reach my hand out, and the girl pulls me up with ease.

"I'll tell you if you tell me how the daughter of Dirge tracked me here."

"Oh, that part's easy." Iron Mask chuckled, draping her cloak back around her and drawing a small storm cloud around her hand to wash the mud from the Iron Mask.

"You are way louder than you think, and I would know the *Stormblade* anywhere. A Reaper ship stopping in Root is rare enough, but two? There's a story to two ships pulling in at the same time, and then your voice just *carries* in the market."

The girl held the mask out at arm's length and admired her cocky grin in its reflection.

"So you're Branch's daughter?" I say, pulse mounting as I look back and forth between the girl and her mask.

"Not exactly. And I'm not Dirge's daughter, either." The girl meets my eyes as she fixes the mask back to her face, beads of rain dripping from the shark's teeth. "You're dealing with the original. *I'm* Dirge. Now, for the third time, why are you here?"

— 23 —

I can see my slack-jawed expression reflected in Dirge's iron mask, her gray eyes alive with silent laughter.

"No, no." I shake my head. "They said that Dirge was a super-soldier, a terrifying tower of meat and metal, a boy made of wings, not . . ."

Dirge sucks her teeth and takes the mask back down, tracing her finger over the tattoo that starts at her temple and ends in feathers near her ear. "Easiest way to disguise the girl behind the legend: Turn it into a poem, then change her to a man. I'd say it works every time, but I've only lived the one life."

"But Branch said . . ." My mind spins as I look at the exact person I've been hunting down—and the spreading bruise that I've put just below the feather tattoo.

"Branch said what they needed to in order to protect me."

"So you two *do* know each other?!" I try not to shout, thinking of how my voice apparently *does* carry as much as Gourd used to complain.

"You're not captain because of your perceptive abilities, are you?" Dirge grunts, tapping her forearm where . . . wait.

"You were a captain?! Why doesn't your Mark of the Scythe glow?!" I'm full of questions as Dirge hushes me.

"So far, you've asked a million questions, and I understand, I am a marvel and fascinating, and handsome, too. But if you don't tell me in the next five minutes what you are doing here and how you learned my name in order to even *ask* Branch where to find me, we can go right back to fighting, and I *will* stop holding back."

We make hard eye contact with each other before a rustling in the trees behind us catches our eyes.

"Who goes there?" Dirge says, wheeling and aiming her crossbow up into the trees.

"Wait." I place my hand on her shoulder. "I think I know who it might be."

I give three hard, short whistles and tap my knives together twice. An elaborate series of knocks answers back.

"Dirge, meet my brother, Moss," I say as Moss slides down the tree trunk to the ground. "Moss, what are you doing out here?"

"Rain said the story she's telling is for grown-ups and to go find you, but then when I came to the room you were gone so I came looking, but then you were fighting this other girl and I didn't want to mess it up so I hid in the tree until you won." He nodded resolutely, as if that settled the matter.

"He's very cute. Nosy but cute." Dirge lowers her crossbow.

Then points it at me. "You have three minutes to begin your story, by the way."

I watch Dirge's eyebrows play up and down while I tell the tale of how I became the captain of the *Moony*. When I get to the part about Sunshower and Chinara of the Shard Reapers being taken, Dirge gasps as if she's been struck.

"They're becoming more aggressive," Dirge mutters, punching her fist into the palm of her other hand. The wood gauntlets on her wrist drum against each other like branches. "So you came to ask me to lead a mission to the Depths?"

I nod, my mouth creasing into a frown. "Who knows how fast the Pointers might move. There may not be the Five Heavens for any of us much longer."

"I'm retired." Dirge frowns. "I was hidden for a reason."

"Who retires at thirteen?!" I interject.

"Fourteen."

"But you came here for a reason, right?" Moss pleads.

Dirge's face softens each time she looks at Moss, and seeing an opportunity, Moss loves to tell a story.

"I'm just saying, you came out here when you could have stayed hidden. We were looking in, like, *all* the wrong places to find you."

"Moss," I rebuke harshly, but he continues.

"I don't know what happened to make you hide. It probably hurt a lot." Dirge flinches slightly but says nothing. "But I guess what Violet and I are trying to say is that her dad is missing, and so is your friend, and Sunshower. And maybe, eventually, a whole lot more people. There aren't many Reapers; we can't afford for there to be fewer. But the Children of the Shark stole *a captain*. It's a crisis."

"There's always a crisis," Dirge responds tersely. "And I told you, I'm retired."

"But *can* you help?"

Dirge's face flits through emotions so fast it almost looks like the wing at her temple is flapping. "Yes. Maybe. Mostly maybe."

"Okay, that I can work with."

"But I am hidden here. I could just knock you out and go back to being hidden." Dirge shrugs, unflinching.

"You could try." I pull a smirk onto my face to emphasize the next words. "You could maybe go back to being hidden, but I would keep searching forever. Because I'm annoying and proud. But also, I saw your expression when I said Chinara had been taken. You seem too smart to think the appetite of sharks can simply be ignored. You can go back to hiding, but soon there will be no land left to hide on if their advance continues."

Dirge grimaces, mouth forming around even more silent calculations before letting out a long sigh.

"The little one is right. I'd have never met you if I'd just stayed on the mango farm."

"Does that mean you'll help?" I ask brightly.

"Does that mean you have mango?" Moss asks, equally bright.

Dirge sticks out her fist for me to bump before saying, "Yes, to both. But I will not be happy about it, and I will not share the strips with chili powder on them. Those are my terms."

When we all step inside the great hall of the farm, a wave of appreciative laughter swallows the sound of our entrance. *Nearly.* Gourd startles to see me coming through the door with rainwater dripping off my clothes and is about to say something, when Rain's booming laugh cuts her off, and she waves at me from the front of the room.

"Violet! I see you got caught in the storm. Didn't you hear they said it was going to rain?!"

"Who said it was going to rain?" says one of the Ropers.

"The sky I guess." Rain guffaws and the audience groans, which only makes her laugh harder.

Gourd rolls her eyes and scans my face in a what-have you-been-up-to kind of way. Her eyes snag on Dirge, who stashes her iron mask under her hooded cloak and avoids eye contact as she stares at the ceiling.

"Oy, are we still getting the final story?" another crew member asks.

Rain finally straightens and wipes a self-satisfied tear from her eye. Wordlessly, she and Gourd scatter their painted sand as they mutter incantations. An abundance of blue and gray spills from their bags, white and maroon sand swirling together to form little shark-headed figures that dance and fight in the wind. I smile despite myself. It's one of my favorites, *the Mother of Teeth*.

"It is said that before the storm, the Mother was mother of nothing." Gourd's voice is honey as blue sands wash over themselves, a small tide hanging in the air. The gathered audience oohs and aahs at the display of color. "A monstrous shark the length of three Reaper ships."

Beneath the fake waters, the gray sands take the form of the Mother of Teeth herself. Her gills shimmer in the flickering light of the candle as the Chainbreakers' ships glide over her waters, unknowing.

"The Mother was mother of nothing, god of sharks and loneliness," Rain continues, "until the day of the storm, until the dawn of the Chainbreakers."

Plumes of black smoke and sandy storm clouds grow dense above the ships. The Chainbreakers seize the decks and control of the ships. The bodies of some of the Chainmakers leap from the tops of the ships, sinking through the fake ocean and into the water.

"The gods of the old world and the new churned the storm above the Chainbreakers' heads. Winds ripped the sky and sang the story of every blade. And beneath it all . . .

"The Mother of Teeth stirred," Gourd and Rain say together ominously.

I look at Gourd and see her wrestling a smile off her face. Rain was right about Gourd. Growing up here, Gourd could never make her life the epic story she wanted to tell.

"The Mother of Teeth rose as the Reaper ships descended to the Tides of the Lost, for she had heard the call of the Storm at the Edge of the World and thought it the growl of another shark, another god."

The huge shark's fin passes swiftly between the Reaper ships, sending waves everywhere. Colored sand flies into the first row of the audience with a splash that leaves half the crew sputtering.

Gourd's voice turns grave. "But instead, all she found was the Chainmakers, and their curses."

Dirge lets out an exasperated sigh that goes unheard by the rest of the crowd. Miniature models of the Chainbreakers become the first Reapers as they pull souls from the water.

"The Chainmakers were too heavy to hoist themselves onto the boats they'd built and lost," Rain continued. "So the Mother of Teeth feasted on them and became the mother of their curse. And in turn, the Chainmakers became the Children of the Shark."

Dirge yawns as the ghost-shark hybrids flee from within the Mother of Teeth and cast themselves to the bottom of the sea and into the Depths.

"Are you bored?" I whisper harshly.

"Yes," Dirge says, as if it should be obvious.

"But I thought they did a good job," Moss chimes in. "It's an interesting myth."

"It'd have to be untrue to be a myth. The Mother of Teeth is no myth; I've seen her."

— 24 —

"So let me get this straight, one last time." Gourd pinches the bridge of her nose as Dirge, Moss, Rain, and I huddle together in the shed where Rain keeps her tilling equipment. "This is the most dangerous Reaper in the Five Heavens?" She points at Dirge, who is leaning backward on a barrel and lazily salutes. Gourd narrows her eyes at the fourteen-year-old-prodigy.

"Not only that," I say, "she's also the only Reaper who can take us on a mission that the council explicitly forbade us from undertaking, with a very low possibility of success and a high chance of death and dismemberment for all involved."

"And this is a fact you would like my help in conveying to the other Reaper ships so they can convene a Captains' Council at Moonpoint Harbor, purely on the basis of your newfound friendship?"

"Ain't nobody said I was her friend," Dirge interjects, peering out the window at the moon.

"Well, what would you define yourself as?" Rain asks helpfully.

Dirge polishes a nonexistent spot off her mask. "An independent contractor protecting the interests of her mango farm, her privacy, and her—"

"So you and your new friend," Gourd interrupts, continuing with her voice slightly raised, "have a plan to assault the Depths."

"*Plan* is such a strong word . . ." Dirge muses.

Rain laughs while Gourd's face hardens.

"All right, Violet, this sounds like a terrible idea, and the folks on your team wouldn't even call it a *plan*. Why would you think I would sign off on this?" Gourd rubs her temples in annoyance.

"Because you heard the idea out three times?" Moss offers, then shrinks at a withering look from Gourd.

"Violet? You're uncharacteristically quiet," Gourd notes.

"Well, it's because I think Moss is right," I say stepping closer to Gourd and meeting her eyes. "You listened to the idea three times. And maybe you would have listened to my first plan if I shared it with you when I came up with it. Maybe Sunshower would still be here, or Chinara for Shard. But we don't know, because they were taken." My voice quivers as memories of their faces flash behind my eyes, and I shut them tight before continuing. "Because I wasn't the leader I should've been. The captain worthy of this ship." I stare at the shimmering Mark, the light pulsing in time with my breath. "I'm sorry. I let you down, and this crew, and the Five Heavens. But I am trying to make it right now. It has been a matter of days, and how many more Reapers have been taken while we have been stranded by the Slavetide? We cannot waste a moment."

Gourd clears her throat and leans back against a precarious-looking stack of wooden buckets.

"Before Dad fell, I thought being captain was about being the hero in a story. But the stories of the past can only be told because we were gifted this place, all of this, to nurture and protect." I gesture around. "Now that a Reaper of legend we were seeking drops from the sky, is this not also a gift? I think we have an opportunity, a real opportunity. And if nothing comes of it, if the other ships will not follow, then we will return to Horizon. But I think you see the gift, too, so I'm coming to you. And whatever you recommend, that's what we'll do. But Sunshower, Chinara, Dad: We owe it to them to try . . . to at least have a meeting about trying." I stare at Gourd, the shadows across her face drawing long black lines beneath her tired eyes.

"If—and it is an *if* as wide as the Tides of the Lost," Gourd says slowly as triumphant smiles snake across my and Moss's faces, "we were to pull this off, we would need the support of all five Reaper ships."

"Shard will likely support you. They're always down for a fight." Rain punches the air.

"Crest will follow; they've wanted an opportunity to study

the Depths for years. Plus, the easiest way into the Depths is via the Fang Waves." Dirge swings her leg over the side of the barrel she's been sitting on.

"Then I will talk with Captain Blues about the *Sagewind* joining the *Moony* in calling a Captains' Council at Moonpoint Harbor."

A day and a half later, Rain bids us farewell with rib-cracking hugs as we step back aboard the *Moony*. By the grace of the gods, I can barely see where the planks have been replaced and healed with new wood from the Star-Drenched Baobab. As soon as I step aboard, I feel a tingle of magic riding under my skin; there's no power like being home.

We check supplies and wave a signal flag for the *Sagewind* to follow, and I urge the *Moony* forward into the clinging fog over the early morning waters. Rain waves from the shoreline, Dirge's three scrolls of directions on how to care for her mango farm spilling from Rain's other hand. I look back over my shoulder as the ship pulls away, increasing in speed as the Heaven of Root grows smaller and smaller in the distance. The elegant curves and lines of the crops thread over the soil like elaborate braids.

"You going to miss it?" Dirge asks, chewing lightly on a long blade of grass as the two of us sit in the crow's nest, taking turns navigating for Mooneye, who wasn't up to using his newly refilled vision bowl.

"Maybe. I guess if this ends up being a doomed mission, I'll never know?" I say wryly.

"Such confidence; you're already making me so grateful that I left my home and my privacy and my books to go as far as humanly possible from the things I like!" Dirge hitches a chipper smile onto her face.

"So why did you disappear for so long? And why mangos?" I ask.

"Uh, because there's only one chance to grow something perfect. Duh." Dirge snorts, but I bridge the gap and lean next to her.

"I'm serious, though. We're about to literally go into the mouth of a shark together. I know why I *have* to go. I think it'd be nice to know why you left."

Dirge spins the long grass between her fingers before whispering a story to the wind, which carries the grass into the water.

"You ever feel like you're a secret to everyone, but you still belong to everyone?" Dirge finally says, not meeting my eyes.

I stroke my chin, my mind drifting back to the image of me in a white sarona at Dad's candle boat ceremony.

"That's why." Dirge sucks her teeth. "When I was younger, actually kinda my whole life, I was a secret people in Shard whispered about in the streets. The prodigy Storm-caller who could bend lightning around her hand. The boy made of wings. The savior of the Five Heavens. You know how it is."

I nod, pretending to know how it is.

"But the problem is, you don't get to be a child when you're the savior; you just get to be the savior. Nobody *knew* who I was or what I looked like. I was kept in the academy since—" Dirge looks around like she's forgotten something, eyes hard. A beat later, she settles for fishing another long blade of grass from her pants pocket and sticking it in her mouth. "Since my parents were killed."

I reach out to touch Dirge's shoulder, but she shrugs away from it and offers a fist bump instead.

"Not big on touching overall, if that's cool?"

"Oh, definitely. My mistake." I rush to apologize.

"Nah, it's cool. You didn't know. But yeah, def more of a talk-it-out type of Reaper. Anyway, I guess what I'm saying is, I barely got a chance to remember Dad, and my mom was killed on a mission out near the Fang Waves a little after I was born. So I never knew much beyond the Chainbreaker family legacy."

My jaw hangs like a broken door.

"Wait, you're . . . ?"

"The great-great-great-granddaughter of one of the first Chainbreakers?" Dirge gives a bored grin.

"It feels like there should be more *greats* in there?" I ask.

"The ships and their memories are never as far behind you as you think," Dirge responds, locking her gray eyes onto mine.

"But yes, that's the legacy I was born into, and I guess I

fulfilled some prophecy about a child who could liberate us all blah-blah-blah, and then my Stormcalling and Tidewatching skills meant I was always in the advanced courses for Reaper training with the adults blah-blah-blah. And I became their ultimate weapon, the blade against the dark. I've been Dirge ever since."

"Dirge isn't your real name?" I ask.

"No, it was actually Whisper, but I've been Dirge for so long, it's become my name, too, in a way." Dirge mumbles a spell into her fingers and a tiny storm cloud orbits her knuckles.

"Which would you prefer?" I hold her gaze for a second.

Dirge cocks her head to the side. "It's been a while since I had to think about it. I guess Dirge, but maybe Whisper . . . from time to time, when it's just us."

"Well, I'm always here if you ever need some one-on-one time."

"Oh, I'm aware . . . you're *a lot*." Dirge deadpans before her face splits into a grin.

"So is Branch the only person in Shard who knows where you went?"

"Far as I can tell. In many ways they were, like, the only person who knew *I* was there. Most people who knew I existed seemed to think of me more like a spear that could talk." Dirge snorts lightly at her own joke.

"Branch saw me, though, helped me fake my death on a mission out in the Fang Waves. And a couple of cargo crate voyages later, I was in Root. I was alone, but I was, like . . . I don't know, I was, like, my own person for the first time."

A quiet moment passes as we tilt our heads back and stare up at the stars. Stars that are stories written in little points of fire, just like us. Finally, I crack the silence.

"You never answered my question: Why are you coming on this mission?"

"Because you hit hard." Dirge's face softens. "Because you're not wrong to be angry, because you're angry for the same reason I am. I've never really had a . . . person, a person my own age. Because I can help you do something about this wild situation before it's too late. Or maybe because I've let my anger make all my choices lately, and all I got was a mango farm I'm getting farther from by the second." She laughs and punches me lightly in the shoulder.

"And you. I guess I got you, too." Dirge finishes, eyes awkwardly fixed on sliding the mini storm cloud along her knuckles again.

"I don't know how you do that, make a storm that small," I tease. "Stormcallers are always so angry, I assumed it's always *tsunami or bust* with y'all."

Dirge giggles and expands the cloud before swallowing it back into her palm. She stands and offers me her hand, pulling me to my feet.

"Say what you will, rage needs a home like anything else. Can't swallow it, can't let it decide for you, either."

I bite my lip, thinking of my mistake with the Slavetide.

"Can you teach me how to find a home for that rage?"

Dirge spins a bolt into her crossbow and binds a little storm to it. "Do you one better; I'll teach you the move that *I* invented."

— 25 —

We are the first two ships to arrive at Moonpoint Harbor, and so we get the benefit of half a day's rest and the chance to watch from the balcony as the clingy morning mist parts around the prow of the *Glasstide*. Well, Dirge and Moss get to watch from the balcony at least, but I have to watch from the docks. Gourd insisted that I should be there to greet each of the captains upon arrival. Which makes sense, it's just *way* colder down here than it would be up there. But either way, say what you will about Palm's Reapers—they know how to make an entrance.

Plumes of violet and teal sand dance in elaborate patterns above the ship and the sound of drums announces its arrival. The mist parts over the prim ash-gray wood of the *Glasstide*, Palm's pale blue Sankofa bird flag proudly flying above it.

Gourd groans.

I turn to ask Gourd if she's feeling ill.

"All of this is so . . . unbecoming."

"I've never seen them on the tides; barely knew they had a ship," I tease.

"Hush," Gourd snaps, fighting back a grin.

"I was quiet," I insist as the gangway of the *Glasstide* docks to the pier and the drums reach a fever pitch. "You're the one who can't stand theatrics."

"Violet," Gourd warns, lip twitching. She raises a finger to say something but thinks better of it before settling for: "Fix your face. We are trying to win allies not a comedy medal."

I huff and hitch a grin onto my face as the captain of the *Glasstide*, a tall woman whose elegant blue box braids match the flag, walks onto the deck. She wears a white robe and a sharkskin belt with a pair of steel rods on each hip. We clasp arms in the traditional captains' greeting, and she extends the same to Gourd, who did an admirable impression of someone with respect for the person they are talking to.

"Captain, I trust the tides were smooth with your journey," Gourd says.

"Oh, here and there." Constellation's voice is high and clear. "We tend to leave the day-to-day reaping to the others. I have so much on my plate governing, as it were."

Gourd's smile covers the clench in her jaw as she says slowly, "And I am sure that the search for your successor will see the *Glasstide* back out on the waters very soon."

"Perhaps." Constellation trains her gaze on me as I draw my shoulders back and try to look the height of a captain. "This situation with the Children of the Shark certainly threatens all that we hold dear in Palm as well as the rest of the Heavens, I'm sure, but—"

I've been around enough adults to sense when one is setting up a veto to a question you haven't even had a chance to ask yet, so instead I clasp Constellation's bejeweled hand in mine.

"Captain, you honor us with your presence. But I'm certain your journey has been long, and I would love to help get you settled in the archive."

Constellation's eyes light up at the idea of going to the rounded room of dusty scrolls from captains' meetings past. But before we have a chance to move, a roar emerges from beyond the veil of mist, the unmistakable sound of the arrival of Crest's Reaper ship, the *Wavetamer*.

"I think we may want to step back a pace or two," Gourd warns as the mist parts like twin columns of smoke and the rudder arms of the *Wavetamer* kick up a high arcing splash.

Right where we just stood is drenched, so, good call by Gourd.

I marvel at the shape of the *Wavetamer*, which is unlike every other Reaper ship. It is shaped like a cross with a shorter body than the *Moony*. A pair of stabilizing arms, controlled from within by a team of elite Windthreaders, manipulates the ship up and down, keeping it from being tossed by the relentless currents of the Fang Waves.

"It's pretty amazing, right?" comes a voice from my right.

I startle seeing Dirge at my shoulder.

"I thought you were watching from upstairs?"

"I was, then I decided to do a different thing." Dirge shrugs.

"And who is this?" Constellation peers at Dirge and then back at me.

"My niece. She's a trainee," Gourd interjects.

"Niece?" I mouth from behind Constellation's back.

"Trainee?" Dirge huffs.

"Ah well, that makes sense. I think I will wait in the archives for dearest Starshadow's arrival. Gourd, would you escort me there, if you please?"

It does not please Gourd, but she begrudgingly takes Constellation's offered elbow as the skeleton crew of the *Glasstide* follow behind with quills and ink but few weapons.

"A whole Heaven of artists and bureaucrats. What could go wrong?" Dirge picks at her teeth.

"Okay, seriously, how did you go all those years without being caught?!" I huff.

Dirge shrugs. "People are less curious after receiving a handful of free mangos."

"You never offered me any mango—"

"And that streak will continue, but hey, here comes my friend, so let's focus on that!"

I stifle a comeback because Dirge is genuinely smiling for the first time in days. I look at the gangway protruding from the *Wavetamer* and see a heavyset boy in a blue dashiki and iron glasses with octagonal lenses riding the wind down off the prow of the ship. In the early morning mist, the light throws dazzling reflections off the silver beads in his braids.

The boy's face splits into a wide grin, and he hustles toward us until Dirge gestures at him to relax, and he falls back into his place behind the procession of Crest Reapers. Their captain is a broad-chested man named Starshadow, who Dad had told me I met as a baby. His long locks are gray at the ends, and his sleeveless leather vest is trimmed with clattering shark teeth as he walks forward and takes my hand with a grin.

"Sister, we are grateful for the call. Though I wish it were under better circumstances. Crest stands with you in taking action. Today and forever."

I blink, a little dumbfounded. I've never had an adult agree with me before I've even had a chance to make a request.

Starshadow beckons me a little closer and leans into my ear. "Your father was like a brother to me. He took in my nephews and made them part of his crew. He will be avenged."

I smile appreciatively. "Or rescued."

"Aye, that's the spirit. May the ancestors guide us to the best winds and the right winds. Now, Captain, I wonder if I might ask something a little unconventional of you?"

I nod as he continues.

"The boy at the back with the goofy grin on his face and beads in his hair?"

I peer down the line at the boy Dirge pointed to earlier,

who is batting one of his own locks in front of his face and trying not to look at Dirge too long.

"His name is Zay. His mother was our Tidewatcher, but she was recently stolen by the enemy like your father. He's very bright . . . He actually helped redesign our ship, but he's been distant since Amira was taken from us. I would mean no insult, but if he could know the company of Reapers his own age, I would be grateful."

A warm feeling courses over my skin as I notice Starshadow hasn't called us children.

Reapers his own age.

"It would be my honor, and I feel I should mention that Constellation is awaiting you in the archives." I salute.

"And no doubt already wishing that she was back home in Palm." Starshadow chuckles, signaling to his crew to follow.

The boy, Zay, peels off and peers around the corner as the rest of the crew files down the hallway. Zay's a half a head taller than me, and now that he is close, I can see he has two pointed silver teeth. He offers Dirge a fist bump, almost bouncing with excitement.

"Violet, this is Zay," Dirge declares. "His brilliance is only exceeded by his lack of subtlety."

"My bad, I just I thought I'd never see you again," Zay says.

"I mean, yes, because you were told that I died, you little fool." Dirge giggles behind her hand.

"Yeah, but it wasn't, like, convincing. Branch told me, but they're not a very good liar."

"It's true. I knew they were lying, too," I say.

"No, you didn't. You didn't know anything until I cornered you!" Dirge corrects.

"Well, yes and no. I had given up hope of finding you, but the only time Branch got emotional, they referred to you as *she* instead of *he*. So that kinda gave it away. And then"—I point a finger at Dirge—"you tried to shoot me. Which . . . definitely made it clearer."

We all laugh, our voices echoing along the dock as the grim outline of the *Stormblade* looms out of the mist. The meeting will begin soon, and above our heads, the stars grow dimmer.

— ✦ 26 ✦ —

It is so quiet in the ancient meeting hall of the first Chain-breakers that I can hear the dust hum. I run my hands over my chair, a dark oak inscribed with the symbol of the moony fish in both armrests. The table is an intricate hand-carved map of the tides, meticulously painted in ceruleans and windy grays. I run my hands along it as the other four Reaper captains file in with their first mates alongside them. Dirge sits at my left hand, scratching at the headwrap of her disguise and thumbing the space of her missing nose ring.

"I just don't understand why I should have to wear this itchy thing if Fog already knows what I look like." Dirge squirms uncomfortably.

"Because," Gourd whispers back sharply, "you are our secret weapon, and I already told Constellation that you were my niece, so we will keep the hat on until I tell you it is time to make your presence known."

The two scowl at each other from either side of me in a

way that does make them genuinely look related as the last of the Reaper captains, a bald, muscular man named Fog, struts in and sits at the lightning-and-blade insignia of Shard.

Gourd rises and raps her ring twice on the edge of the table for attention as the din of side conversation dies down.

"Friends, Reapers, Siblings of the Tides, you honor us by honoring our call." Gourd's voice is stiff and formal, none of the theatrical storyteller she was the other night as she made a sand model of the Mother of Teeth.

"The hour is dire, and none of us can deny it. Each of our ships has lost crew members. I speak on behalf of our captain, who has convinced me we cannot rely on the Children of the Shark to play by the rules that have governed our war for centuries. We must take decisive action."

"Not all our ships have lost crew. The *Stormblade* and Shard have taken on more risk than any other." Fog's voice is gravel over sea glass, low and sharp, as he glares across the table at Constellation.

"Some of us have had governance to attend to rather than continuing an endless war with Pointers," Constellation hisses, the Sankofa bird symbol of Palm glittering on her shoulder.

"Some of us realize the war chose us already, glass-sail," Fog growls back before Branch places a hand to his shoulder, and he relaxes back into his seat.

Dirge nudges me in the ribs, and I lean back to hear her. "Chinara was Fog's partner. Without her, he does not seem himself."

I bite my lip, nodding as I tune back in to the conversation.

"Regardless," says Blues, captain of the *Sagewind*, stroking his long brown beard, "we cannot answer an attack by the Pointers with inaction."

"I just fail to see how an all-out assault on the Depths is even possible, let alone the *best* plan." Constellation crosses her arms to a heavy snort from Fog.

He retorts, "What wisdom would a Palm Reaper see in a plan that involved something besides talking?"

"I have something to say." I rap my fist on the ancient table for quiet.

A hush falls over the room as Fog folds his arms and leans back skeptically to whisper something to Branch, whose eyes are trained on Dirge.

I rise to my feet and lean over the table.

"Each of us has lost something to the Children of the Shark. But we still have an opportunity to fight." I look at Constellation. "I have not asked you here to call for a war. I'm asking for us to end the one that has already been waged on us since before my birth." I tap my hand in the middle of the carved map and meet Zay's eyes over Starshadow's shoulder. "Since the birth of the tides."

Fog rises in his seat. "More work that falls to the *Stormblade*, more risk that falls to the *Stormblade*, and who will sing our songs when my Reapers pay the price for your plans?"

"Brother Fog, is it not the dream of Shard to ride into the Depths?" Starshadow asks, confused. "Is that not why Shard and my people in Crest have shared information on the Fang Waves for generations?"

"It has been," Branch answers, one eye still trained on Dirge, who looks like she has eaten a sour plantain.

"It still is," Fog insists, then sneers at the Palm Reapers. "At least *some* of us want to rid the tides of the enemy. But we cannot be asked to shoulder so much of the burden."

Constellation is on her feet, hand near the batons at her belt in an instant.

"You speak as if we have no care for the Passengers. Who maintains a life for them that is not at the end of a blade? Palm. If the *Glasstide* is not there to protect Palm, who secures our shores? Who looks after our future? You? A joke. We will not break our ship for that. There are no cowards in this room. And if bruises are requested, I will oblige the honorable Shard captain in his wish," she hisses.

A thick vein pulses in Fog's neck as he pushes his chair back.

"After generations, finally, you lot show some fight? Where were you days ago when the Pointers stole my love? You would follow this girl with half a ship and no plan?"

"You will speak of her," Gourd growls, every eye shifting to her, "with respect, or I will claim that interrupting tongue myself."

The volume of the airing of old feuds rises further as I meet Zay's eyes. We both glance down at the map as arguing shadows stretch over every corner, every Heaven.

Don't they understand there's no time for this? I think.

Don't they realize the old world is gone?

And as if in answer, I hear the softest roll of thunder, and above our heads a miniature storm cloud spirals and lets loose a velvet rain. Dirge rises beside me as the voices of the elders and captains quiet and removes her hat. The *Stormblade* Reapers, living and dead alike, gasp at her gleaming wing tattoo.

"What trickery is this?" Constellation asks, befuddled.

"No trick," Dirge says flatly, brushing rainwater from her shoulders. "I am Dirge of Shard. And I have been gone too long, running from what faces us. But each of us came here because all along the waters, you sense it." Dirge's whisper pulls everyone closer as all the hair on my arms stands to listen.

"The dullness in the water is rising from below. The world we have defended since the first Chainbreakers, since my ancestors first laid eyes on this place and saw nothing but water and a world free of the threat of the Chainmakers, is gone."

A rumble of hushed gossip circles the table. Dirge looks at me expectantly, and I step into her place.

"Dirge and I have a plan to summon the Mother of Teeth

to ride down to the Depths, but it will require all of your help."

"You mean to tell us your plan hinges on a children's story?" mutters Constellation.

Dirge rolls her eyes before coughing to try and cover it. "I mean to tell you our plan hinges on a legend."

"Let the girl finish," Fog growls.

"You're on her side now?" Constellation gasps.

"She has found a daughter of one of the Chainbreakers we'd thought lost to us. If anyone can—" Fog's voice falters briefly before continuing. "If she has found Dirge, then there is still hope."

"I don't know a Dirge." Constellation brushes the comment aside. "But if all our ships are lost in a doomed mission, who will keep our shores for the Passengers? Nobody else here is thinking about the future."

Maybe I haven't thought this through? What if I lose everyone, like I lost Sunshower, and the Moony, *and—*

Dirge's hand slides into mine and gives it a brief squeeze. I did bring her back here, a legend they said could not be found. I've made friends of myths before. Warm weather blooms in my chest as I clear my throat again for silence.

"Constellation makes a point. I cannot lie, friends, and say that I know any more about the hell I am asking your help in finding than you do. I am a daughter of the Five Heavens. All I have known is this ceaseless cycle of the Children of the

Shark stealing Passengers, and now they have taken the only family that I thought remained to me."

The quiet hums again as I pause, surveying the room while Zay draws his fingers in the air ahead of him like he's doing some mental math.

"No matter the brightness of the moon or the sharpness of the blade, the Children of the Shark come. They have come since the days of the Archer of a Hundred Promises and the Star-Drenched Baobab. Because they were born of the Mother of Teeth, the Children of the Queen of Hunger wear her name."

I jab my finger at the Fang Waves on the carved map between us all, then draw my finger back to Moonpoint Harbor.

"The Children of the Shark hunt us in death and life. Their appetite was always going to grow beyond Passengers. We know because it has been hundreds of years. And still, we have survived because we are the children of the Chainbreakers."

A low buzz of chatter follows, murmurs of agreement echoing off the walls as Dirge begins to pound a slow beat on the table, and others join until the whole room is a drum and I call above the beating.

"Are we not the children of survival? Of the Sun People, who prayed to the gods of the sky and the strength of their hands? Are we not the children of those who said *No more*? Who tore the chains from their wrists and made their Heaven where they were?"

A roar of agreement goes up, even the Palm Reapers taking the beat now as I feel myself stand taller, my voice strong and vibrant.

"All our legends begin with the hands of legends not yet named, prayers not yet answered. The Chainbreakers didn't have the luxury of knowing they would become the Chainbreakers; they only knew the stars were dim."

"From the mouths of the young!" Blues smacks the table hard in assent as the pounding beat grows in volume beneath my words, building to a crescendo.

"Our legends begin with a dimming of the stars. Siblings, our enemy gathers below us."

A great cry shakes the dust from the shelves, the whole room vibrating as my fellow Reapers stand united, stomping their feet in agreement. Even Constellation has taken up the pounding.

"Children of the Chainbreakers, if our stars are dim, it is only because the ancestors trust that we will fight in the dark."

Beneath the stars, all five Reaper ships churn over the black glass of the water, leaving white waves in our wake on the way to Zay's workshop in Crest. Zay and Dirge join me on the prow of the *Moony*, leaning on either side of me. Normally I like being alone, but a warmth spreads through my chest as the biting cold of the water dots my cheeks.

"Violet, you were incredible back there!" Zay beams, the moonlight winking in the silver beads braided into his hair.

"Me? What about you?" I blush as Dirge rolls her eyes.

As the din of the meeting chamber had settled down after my speech, I laid out Dirge's and my full plan. We would need to re-create the Storm at the Edge of the World to draw out the Mother of Teeth and attach a small Reaper ship to her fin to ride down with her into the Depths. A team of Windthreaders would be able to cast a bubble of air to allow us to breathe underwater, and then we would escape from the back of the shark when we reached the lair that Dirge had seen on her last mission. Constellation and Blues had been wary about the prospect of combining the ships together, and I worried the alliance was about to fall apart all over again.

But then Zay had spoken, and I'd expected the captains and their crews to laugh it off, to treat him like, well, a fellow kid. But even the other Reaper clans' captains had fallen back to listen to Zay explain the magical physics and how portions of the *Moony, Glasstide, Stormblade, Wavetamer,* and *Sagewind* could be combined into one smaller ship.

"Half the tides know that Zay is a genius." Dirge smirks proudly. She holds out the crossbow on her wrist and stares down the sight. "He's the one who built me this!"

"And you're the one who didn't oil it the way I told you to."

"Death made me forgetful." Dirge shrugs, unstrapping the light wood gauntlet from her wrist and holding it out to me.

"Oh, I couldn't accept that." My eyebrows nearly fly off my face at Dirge offering me her signature weapon.

"No worries, because I was definitely not offering for keeps." Dirge ties the straps around my free wrist and pulls the leather to a tight knot that makes my fingers tingle. "I told you I'd teach you my signature move, and now we are riding into the mouth of a literal shark to take us to a world full of demons."

"Oh, that makes way more sense! I've never really done Stormcaller magic."

"Well, start by telling the wind a story to load the bolt

in and then aim off to—" Dirge scans the deck before Zay points portside.

I aim where they point and whisper a small story that loads the bolt with a satisfying click.

"Now, I want you to touch that anger inside you."

"But I'm not angry right now." I smile awkwardly.

"Yes, you are. You've been angry the whole time I've known you, and you should be. You're afraid of how angry you actually are all the time, and the one moment you let it out, it cost you somebody close to you."

I shut my eyes briefly and push Sunshower's face away.

"There, see! That!" Dirge points to my chest. "I was watching you a good long time before we fought. Your anger is something you push down, push away, but it radiates from you. I told you rage needs a home like anything else. So give it a home at the edge of this bolt; push the fury through it, and watch it explode."

I chew my lip and swallow hard.

I close my eyes and let my mind flow down my arm and along the silvered tip of the crossbow bolt. I reach for the hot prickle that often forms in my gut but find nothing. I take another breath and think of Dad's face, Sunshower's face, and feel the rage flare to my fingertips.

"Good, don't lose that thread. I can see the lightning at your fingertips. Press deeper, find what hurts," Dirge insists in my ear.

The faces of the lost blur together in my mind, the watery flames from my first dream about Dad roaring to life before them until they are only shadows.

What if we never get them back? What if they're lost forever?

My eyes snap open to find a storm growing at my fingertips. I reach out to the trembling tip of the bolt and gingerly cup my hand around it. Tiny storm clouds orbit the point until I let loose the bolt and watch the singing arrow explode into rain over the roiling waters.

"Good. Very good." Dirge nods with approval.

"Sometimes we fear our anger because our anger comes from fear," Zay notes, staring up at the sky and the dimming stars.

"That's wise. You really are a genius." I grin, assessing the device on my arm.

"It's a thing my mom used to say." He kicks at the deck as the smile slides from my face.

"I'm so sorry; I didn't know."

Zay pulls his eyes down from the stars to look at me and gives a sad smile. "Don't be; we're about to build the ship that brings her back. Nothing to be sorry for. We just have to win."

The voice in my head still doubts it, but instead of pushing it away, I take a deep breath and clap Zay on the shoulder.

"Then I have only one question for you: Does this crossbow come in black?"

This time Zay's grin isn't sad. It's all teeth, and his silver ones make it look like he has taken a bite out of the moon.

It turns out the crossbow isn't the only thing that comes in black. Zay's workshop in Crest is a huge messy space next to the harbor. He directs various crew and captains on where to bind the final pieces of the new ship. It is pitch-black with the different elements of the five Reaper ships—each of them except the *Moony*, which is of course why I'm here.

"The *Moony*'s wood ought to be the final piece," says Zay, stroking his chin proudly.

"Just tell me where to press and transfer!"

"In a moment. I have a surprise for you." Zay waves an engineer over, who carries a case gingerly and hands it to Zay.

I cock an eyebrow, but he simply hands me the case.

Inside are two gauntlets just like Dirge's, one with a crossbow attached to the top. They are a beautiful rose-oak. I lift one carefully from its case.

"Well, you don't have to be *that* gentle with them. They are for combat after all."

"They're gorgeous." My voice is barely above a whisper.

Zay beams with pride, mouth open to begin an excited explanation before I continue.

"And I don't mean to sound ungrateful . . ." Zay's smile falters a little. "But why are there two of them? Just because I have two arms?"

Zay's smile turns mischievous, and he gestures for me to try them on. Once I've done that, Zay tells me to call my Thousand Knives to me. When I do, twin curved blades of wind erupt from each side.

"A Reaper needs her scythes, especially the captain of . . ." Zay beams, staring at his inventions proudly before signaling an engineer near the prow of the new ship.

The engineer salutes back and cuts loose a bit of fabric to reveal gold letters painted on the hull.

The Chainbreaker.

"The gauntlets didn't come in black but—"

His words are lost as I pull him into a tight hug that he returns.

The next morning, everything is in place as the crews of the now six Reaper ships flow forward to the edge of the Fang Waves. The whitecaps of the waves give the water teeth.

I stare from the bow of the *Chainbreaker*, small and dark against the tides, as Mooneye stands at the prow of the next ship, the *Moony*. My original Mark of the Scythe dimly glows on his arm. He looks nervous, as we all do.

Soon the second layer of storm rises from the voices of the Stormcallers and the Windthreaders of Palm, and Root adds their voices until the storm is a choir, causing the glow of the Children of the Shark's ships to flare beneath the water.

My crew is made up of Gourd, Dirge, Zay, two expert

Windthreaders from Palm, including Constellation's first mate, Scroll, and of course Moss, who refused to be left behind no matter how much Gourd pleaded. The storm builds as the sickly green color spreads beneath the turbulent water.

And then the glow disappears. The Children of the Shark scatter, and their mother breaches the surface of the Fang Waves. The Mother of Teeth's roar eclipses the storm, her eyes hungry and wide as the moon.

— 28 —

Millions of buckets of water slide down the back of the Mother of Teeth as she thrashes toward the surface, her fangs nearly the height of the *Stormblade*. In the flashes of lightning, I can see scars the length of entire Reaper ships lining her body and that a large portion of the deadly shark-god's fin has been torn.

"What could scar something that—" Moss asks, but a tremble beneath the water interrupts as the green glow of the enemies' ships passes beneath us like lantern fish.

"They're headed for the other Reapers," Zay calls, pointing as the spots of light make their way to the *Glasstide*.

The first Pointer rockets out of the water. I gasp as I see more hooks emerging, threatening to pull the Reaper ship sidelong.

Could a Reaper ship capsize? I wonder, mind stretching back toward the nausea of the Slavetide making contact with the *Moony*.

My gut roils as thunder groans above us, and I see one of the Pointers sprint toward the *Glasstide*'s mast. Its comrades clamor below, battling hand to hand with the Palm Reapers, but nobody seems to have noticed the pearl-white body of the Pointer making its way to the mast as the Mother of Teeth's bellow swallows the sound of the thunder. If Sunshower were here, he could have shot it down, but Dirge's and my crossbows don't have that kind of range.

My stomach drops as it all falls into place. The Pointer wants to please its god. It will tear the sails, stranding the *Glasstide* with the beast I summoned headed right for it.

I feel my mind begin to pull the *Chainbreaker* toward the other ship, my new gray and gold Mark of the Scythe tattoo begging me forward to meet the old enemy, to save a new ally. But my breath catches in my chest as I feel Gourd's palm on my shoulder. I expect her to chastise me, for her brows to knit together in doubt, but instead she points to the *Glasstide* again with a knowing look. I follow her gaze and see—

"Yo," Dirge calls to me, handing me a telescope that I press my eye to.

"Constellation is kicking butt!" I yelp.

Palm's Reaper captain may be an old bureaucrat, but she's a terror with her twin batons, spinning them in a silver blur between her fingers and somehow steering her ship from danger all at the same time. She catapults up on a plume of wind, blue box braids splayed out behind her like the wings of a Sankofa bird. Constellation jams the luminous sticks into the mast, stopping right above the Pointer. The demon freezes in shock before she kicks down hard at its nose. I want to keep watching, but the Mother of Teeth roars until the air trembles and my focus snaps back to my own ship.

"They trust us to do our task; let us trust them to do the same." Gourd pats my shoulder as the Mother of Teeth lets loose another roar that chills the marrow in my bones.

I bark orders for everyone to get in position and give Zay leave to send the signal for Phase Two. A yell of assent rises from the other ships as Starshadow and the *Wavetamer* zip forward and catch the eye of the confused and bellowing god of the sharks. She sees the ship and turns in a great tidal wave of muscle to give chase. I urge the *Chainbreaker* forward, hoping that Zay's engineering will prevent the Fang Waves from overturning the ship altogether.

"Come on, come on," I growl beneath my breath, digging deeper and feeling the ship leap forward in response while the Windthreaders prepare the chain to latch onto the Mother of Teeth.

The *Wavetamer* takes a hard left and circles back to the edge of the Fang Waves as the Mother of Teeth gives chase, and we scurry to keep up. And then a second enormous fin emerges from the water. For a moment, the Mother of Teeth is frozen, confused, her enormous eyes flitting between the ships and the approaching fin. Could there finally be another like her? An end to her loneliness after all this time? In the eye of the Storm at the Edge of the World, with the Mother of Teeth glaring at ships overrun with her children and the Reapers who have battled them for centuries, in the midst of it all, I give the signal to begin Phase Three.

The wooden fin of the decoy shark that Zay designed dives back beneath the water just as the Windthreaders fire the chain of the grappling hook toward the scarred dorsal fin of the Mother of Teeth. The Reapers of the *Sagewind* and *Glasstide* will their winds to direct the thick chain around the surging shark's fin. When it snaps into place, the *Chainbreaker* is hauled length by length onto the back of the shark, who roars with anger. The deck rumbles over a wave of muscle as the shark prepares to dive.

NOW! I bellow internally, my Windthreader magic flaring in my veins as we begin telling the wind an old story to form the bubble of air around ourselves. Gourd, Scroll, Dirge, Zay, and I hold our hands before us as the winds stir to our cause and thunder slams against our eardrums. It is a short story. The wind does not need to hear much to decide to protect us, the Reapers of the Five Heavens, the first crew of the *Chainbreaker*.

Preserve us. Preserve us. Preserve us.

We chant as the bubble of air forms around us.

Preserve us. Preserve us. Preserve us.

I look at Moss, huddled near my feet, his mouth wide. Even with no magic of his own, still he adds his voice to ours as the great shark goes after the decoy. She dives beneath the water, fleeing from the second Storm at the Edge of the World, the deception of the god of sharks.

And then, with a great wrenching of metal against metal, the tail of the Mother of Teeth erupts from the water, snapping one of the stabilizing arms of the *Wavetamer*. A hideous crunch of wet wood rings out amid the storm as the Reaper ship leans precariously to one side. For a moment the chant stops, and my fellow Reapers watch in horror as the shark prepares to dive and launch again. Zay barrels toward the railing, eyes desperate. I put my arms around his waist and pull him back as a savage wave from behind the enormous shark descends toward us. All the while the Mother of Teeth thrashes, her roar bullying the thunder.

I want to urge the ship forward. I want to tell Zay that we will leave no one stranded. But we also need to restart that windbubble spell immediately or the Mother could pull us down beneath the waves and we will drown before we ever reach the Depths. Then all of this, everyone we have lost, would be for nothing. Despair squeezes cold fingers around my heart, when I feel Zay's body tense in my arms. Not with a sob, though, with a cheer. I blink and see all the proof I need that the ancestors are on our side.

The crew of the *Wavetamer* has unflinchingly split into two groups. One stands at the wounded starboard side of their ship, anchoring ropes for the second group of Windthreaders who have plunged toward the waves in one smooth motion. They race to climb aboard the floating arm, and as soon as the first Windthreader finds purchase on the wood, they are already calling on the wind to push the enchanted wood closer to the ship. The decoy shark banks hard left, and the Mother of Teeth surges to follow, sending a tidal wave up in its haste that threatens to crush everything beneath it. I hear Zay chanting barely above a whisper.

"We fall down, but we get up. We fall down, but we get up," he repeats until my voice joins him, the words humming in our bones.

Two more Windthreaders join the first just in time to channel a jaw-rattling burst of wind that splits the tidal wave in two. The *Wavetamer*'s crew give a cheer that even the storm can't quiet as the steering arm of the ship rides the wave back toward its people. Starshadow can just barely be seen at the prow, eyes glowing a deep green. The *Wavetamer*'s severed part melds seamlessly back into the frame of the ship as the Windthreaders are hauled to safety. A bone-chilling roar shakes the waters as the Mother of Teeth finally understands that the second shark is a decoy. Our chant begins again, and the Mother of Teeth bares her fangs, the ripple of muscle in her back signaling that she is about to dive down and away from this trap.

Preserve us. Preserve us. Preserve us.

The chant grows in my body until I can feel the magic humming along every hair on my arms and in every bone in my body. The Mother of Teeth wails in distress as she breaches again, searching for a second shark to end her lone-liness, again disappointed.

Preserve us. Preserve us. Preserve us.

We convince the wind as the last rains fall to the deck and the chain pulls taut, begging the Mother of Teeth to take us down. Down into the waters, down into the Depths, down to where there may be no return.

Down to Dad, and all our lost, I think. *But what if he isn't there? What if he is already lost?*

I feel a pang in my chest, but it is not yesterday's pain. Yesterday's grief. I look above, and the skies are choked with storm clouds. Against all odds, I laugh as another rumble of muscle shakes the deck, and the Mother of Teeth prepares to pull the *Chainbreaker* down under the waters a final time.

What if the tides were turned to sugar?

The sound of the battle fades in the rush of the waters past our bubble of wind.

What if all the rains led us home?

A yell of assent goes up from the crew as the Mother of Teeth drags us deeper, deeper, and deeper.

What if we leashed a shark as old as the world? What if this is our time? What if all our lost ones are not lost to us? I think at the prow of the ship, my ship.

Millions of bubbles streak above as the Mother of Teeth carries us to the Depths, and in the inky black of the water surrounding us, each bubble is a dim star we pass beneath.

— 29 —

The waters on the path into the Depths are opaque, lit only by flashes of lantern fish as the leviathan shark thrashes her way deeper still in the ocean. We fight to steady ourselves, the muscles of her back shifting beneath us like enormous serpents. Once the air begins to run low, Dirge points to an opening in the rocky caves nearby. I give the signal to detach the chain securing us to the Mother of Teeth. The surging water of her furious dive slingshots us backward with a jolt. I grit my teeth against the force of the water and urge the ship forward into a cave near the top of our hell, the Depths.

The cave that Dirge helps navigate us to is faintly lit. The air smells murky, but it is at least, y'know, air. Luminous corals cast long shadows as we anchor the ship and I task Scroll and her companion, Ayo, with guarding it in case there's a patrol of Pointers.

Ayo nods, her nose rings flashing an eerie blue.

"How will you find your way back to us?" Scroll asks, jaw jutting out.

I step over to the cave wall and place my hand on the damp surface. I close my eyes, letting my mind flow to my fingertips, searching and prodding until finally I feel the faintest dot of Tidewatcher magic flicker behind my eyes.

"The halls of the cave will be hazy, but I can see the way out, I think." I blink, letting my eyes readjust to the low cave light.

"So you two and Moss will stay back and—"

"I will not!" Moss says a little too loudly, to a withering glare from both Gourd and Dirge.

"Moss, you don't have to prove anything." I soften my voice and signal him to lower his.

"I will not be left behind. I won't!" Moss's voice is lower, but still furious and insistent.

"We don't have time for this tantrum. The enemy could be converging back on this position as we speak," Gourd hisses.

"Moss." Dirge's voice is the softest I've ever heard it as she kneels at his side and he turns his round face to her. "This battle is no place for a child, eh?"

"Aren't you a child, too?" Moss's eyes narrow.

"Yes, but I have a lot of years of combat training. And think how sad Violet would be if something happened to you," Dirge says calmly.

Moss looks to me, his chest heaves up and down with emotion. "I will not be left behind. I can help."

"Help how?" Gourd pinches the bridge of her nose, eyes anxiously scanning the cavern for enemies.

"I can see things you can't." Moss stamps his foot. "Hear things you can't. What if you go somewhere that only a Passenger would be able to understand, huh?" Moss wheels to face Dirge as Zay sidles over from checking on the ship's hiding place. "I know Violet would be sad if something happened to me. But couldn't something also happen to me here?"

I look over the group, pulse pounding against my temples like someone is trying to juice my brain. Finally, I kneel before Moss and breathe heavily.

"Moss Chainbreaker, you make a good point, and I would be honored if you would fight by our side." I extend my fist for him to bump, and Dirge does the same.

We make our way through the caves of the Mother of Teeth's lair with me, Gourd, and Dirge at the front while Zay and Moss bring up the rear. Since Dirge is the most prodigious Tidewatcher ever born, she takes the lead through the narrow path while Gourd's stare burns a hole in the back of my head.

"Gourd, if you have something to say about Moss coming along, I feel like we should maybe talk about it while we're in the quiet part of enemy territory?" I finally break down and ask.

"Quiet? Gourd has been breathing as loudly as a war horn

for twenty-five minutes!" Dirge quips from the front of the line, fingers tracing the slimy rock face.

"It is your decision to make, but I would have left the child behind where he would be safe. Why drag him into the heart of danger, to face the very creatures who live to steal him? It is like bringing krill into the mouth of a whale. And now I am the only adult on the mission."

"We're all in danger down here no matter what, and we all knew the risks."

"Knew the risks?" Gourd scoffs as we duck under a series of dripping stalactites. "None of us know anything about what we'll face. We don't know what's out there."

"Something big." Dirge's tone is grave, and she stops moving before kneeling at one of the pools of water near the cave wall.

"How big are you talking?" Gourd and I ask almost simultaneously as Zay and Moss catch up behind us.

"Bigger than the Mother of Teeth, maybe? The echo feels . . . slippery when I can get a bead on it. Just huge, big enough that we haven't yet invented words for how big it is." Dirge's brows knit together in concern as she closes her eyes. "I've been tracking something as we came through the caves. It felt like it's just on the other edge of this little expanse, but then it's gone again. An echo that kinda—It just feels *wrong*."

"Well, we are hunting the Children of the Shark after all," I offer, skin prickling as Dirge shakes her head.

"No, this is something different. I don't think the Children of the Shark are the decision-makers here. I haven't thought so for a while, but this confirms it."

"What does?" Zay asks, adjusting his glasses.

"In Shard, we were taught a theory that there is a Pointer general that hasn't revealed itself. But I can feel the Pointers in the next chamber." Dirge's voice chills.

"Wait, go back to that first part?" I ask, thinking of the huge Pointer that killed Mom when I was small. Bile rises to the top of my throat. But Dirge doesn't hear me, still deep in thought as she touches the water again.

"The Depths is a volcanic trench on the other side of a thin bridge we're about to pass over. Once we get into the central chamber, there will be a huge spire of rock that is connected by bridges to the walls. It looks like there's some kind of chamber system inside. If our friends are anywhere, I'd suggest we start there." Dirge's voice is thin as if she is about to gag.

"Can you feel anyone in the chambers?" I ask.

"Can't tell. You know how normally Tidewatching feels like everything is illuminated and connected? This feels like I'm looking at everything through thick warped glass." Dirge gulps hard, fighting the nausea back down. "There's a huge reservoir of Slavetide running through the entire pit, so I can't see what's waiting for us inside. Just the general outline of a huge chamber of volcanic rock and three large chambers that all seem to be part of one entrance, one exit back out into the pit."

"By the gods, that is strange. It sounds like a vertical maze." Gourd spits onto the ground.

"Not even the strangest part. There's something at the bottom. Sometimes it feels alive and sometimes not, but whatever it is, it's in . . ." Dirge closes her eyes, and I can tell she's trying to reach deeper into the trench, when she withdraws her hand from the water, wincing as if she's been burned. "Unfathomable pain."

Dread floods my chest, chilling my bones. The questions are out of my mouth before I can stop them. "Do you think it's my dad? Or the other captives?"

Dirge shakes her head, looking almost green in the faint light. "The only way to know will be to cross the bridge into the central chamber on the other side of this." She points behind her.

"Then there's no time to waste." I start forward, but Dirge catches my shoulder lightly.

"It's a narrow bridge, and under it is . . . Well, you know how when you were a youngling, you'd lie awake and wonder where all the Pointers went at night?"

"I truly hate that I am nodding in agreement to this," Gourd says.

"I truly hate what you're about to say next," Zay adds.

"And I truly hate that beneath this narrow bridge, there is a river of Children of the Shark."

Grim surprise registers on all our faces as Dirge draws a diagram in the dirt.

"We'll need to stay single file, no noise of any kind. If they sense us, we'll be surrounded on both sides before we can blink."

Moss raises his hand. "What if they look up?"

"Then they will see us. And we will all need to run very, *very* fast." Dirge grimaces.

We walk single file along the thin strip of blackened rock over the white river of Pointer soldiers. The only noise in the cave is the steady drip of water falling from the rocks above. I've never seen a sleeping Pointer before, and I have no plans to do so now, so I try to keep my eyes on my feet as first Dirge, then Gourd, then me, Moss, and finally Zay inch our way over our slumbering enemies.

Gourd and Dirge are already across and beckoning me forward when I hear three sharp clicks. Moss's and my secret signal from back when we chased down Sand through the streets of Horizon, which feels like years ago now.

Wait, three sharp clicks means danger.

My stomach drops out of my body as I turn, looking for Moss and see that he's safe, but Zay is teetering as he fights for balance on the bridge.

"Oh no," I whisper as Moss silently pleads with me to do something before Zay falls.

I waste no time. I pick up Moss and move him to my other side and point him to run to Gourd and Dirge, whose eyes are wide with terror as Zay's fight for balance has sent a rock spinning down toward the river.

At any moment, one Pointer will wake, then another, and another . . . Disaster.

I whisper a story to the wind and feel the magic stir in response as I shape the wind into a pair of hands: one to catch Zay, the other to race and catch the rock. My vision narrows as I hold my breath. By the grace of the gods, Zay finally becomes balanced again, and I see the wind halt the falling rock and place it gently down near the milky river of shark-demons.

Zay and I walk hand in hand to the other side, where Dirge pulls us in for a hug. Gourd punches my shoulder triumphantly and gives Moss a congratulatory smile as we all step gingerly into the utter darkness of the tunnel that leads into the Depths, our enemies none the wiser.

When we finally step out of the darkness to look into the pit that comprises the Depths, I realize we could have guessed every day for a hundred years and still maybe never have gotten close to accurately describing this chamber. It's big enough to fit two Mothers of Teeth in it. The pit is all black igneous rock aside from the rickety wooden bridges that run in and out of a bold central column of stone, dark and mirrored like glass. The walls snake with rust-colored vines and leaves that spread out and up from the dark center of the pit. The Depths' bottom is wreathed in shadows, absent of even the eerie green light of coral.

But worst of all are the faces.

At the end of each bridge, there's a giant face made of

rushing water frozen in agony. The mouths are open wide, large enough for a person to fit through.

"I count three." Gourd squints.

"Same. I think we should take some time to regroup and figure out what these water masks are. Strategize from there?" I say, looking to the group for agreement.

And everyone nods except for Moss. Moss, my boy of smoked glass, Moss Moon, Moss Chainbreaker, hasn't noticed the rusty flower near his feet and how it flutters open with a screech, then snaps shut its chain around his ankle.

Moss makes eye contact with me for just a second before the chain yanks him along the bridge.

And all of us are sprinting after Moss across one bridge and down another. Moss's face is a mask of terror as he claps his hand over his mouth to keep from screaming and sounding the alarm as the chain hauls him through the mouth of the first water mask's frozen scream.

We waste no time, drawing our weapons and running into the silently screaming maw, eyes closed against the water and ready for war. And on the other side, heat spills across my face, light hammers my eyes, and my friends' voices disappear in the rush of the water.

When I open my eyes, I am dry and alone. I stand in the courtyard of a shattered fortress. I look up and feel the sun for the first time.

— 30 —

I throw my hands up to shield my face from the light as the sun bears down on me.

Where am I?

My eyes pulse as they adjust to the light. A cracked and broken fortress surrounds me, chunks of white stone floating up and down as if all the rubble is suspended in water. The sun beams harshly over everything, and in the distance beyond the courtyard, I can see the surface of the water— blue, endless, and quiet at the shoreline. Worst of all, though: no Moss, no Gourd, no Zay, no Dirge.

"I'm alone?" I say, my voice tasting the salty air.

No sooner are the words out of my mouth than the stone around me trembles and re-forms into walls, hemming me in. The fortress knits itself back together, and I am plunged into darkness. From the shadows, a voice deep and wet rumbles in my skull.

"Drowned child, you trespass," it says.

I sink into a fighting stance as small torches flicker to life, and the filthy cobblestones are illuminated.

"WHO SAID THAT?!" I yell, fighting to keep my voice firm.

"*Mine is the parched kingdom, palace of no escape. You are nothing and no one,*" says a slithering voice.

My fists ball tighter as more torches flare up beyond me, leading to a dark wood door.

"Well, that's not ominous at all." I sigh, sounding like Dirge. Speaking of which:

"What have you done with my friends, demon? Tell the truth!" My voice echoes back to me, but nothing else.

Anger flares in my gut. I feel magic rushing through my veins to meet the fury.

"I said, WHERE ARE MY—"

"*Through the door and at the waters, your friends are waiting for you,*" says a second voice, high and sweet. It feels like the voices are so near, like fingernails running along my skin, but I see no one near me.

"Who is this? Enough tricks. Where are my friends? I will not ask again."

"*Through the door,*" the too-sweet voice says. "*There are no answers in the dark, only rot. They are waiting for you in the water. You must hurry. Hurry, or they will*—" The voice disappears in an instant.

Behind me, the stones of the fortress's hallway have shifted and formed a dead end. The stench of death claws sharply at my nostrils. The only way out of this place must be through that door. It wasn't there seconds before in the flickering candlelight as the twin voices slithered around me. But still, when I try to step forward, my feet feel like they're made of lead. I need to take a second to think.

Something about the too-sweet voice feels cavity-inducing and turns the nausea in my stomach like Slavetide. That door just screams it's a trap; only a fool would pass through it.

But there's no other way out.

I step forward, pull the door open, and emerge into a chamber that's identical to the last one. Like I went through a door only to return to the same room I just left.

Again, the slithering voice hisses. It repeats, "*You are owned. You are owned. You are owned.*"

I try to push the voice away. I squint at my surroundings, looking for a way out. Once my eyes adjust, I see a dark wood door, identical to the one in the previous chamber.

But a second later, I realize there are two more doors identical to the first!

"Now what kind of—" I start to wonder but am interrupted by the too-sweet voice, crooning from everywhere in the chamber.

"*What is taking you so long? Don't you miss the water, child?*"

"Of course I do, but—" I start.

"*I can bring you to the kiss of the sun again, all your friends in the sun forever. You need only choose the right door.*"

"Those weren't the rules. There was only one door before.

Return my friends now and show yourself." I stamp my foot as the candles flicker.

It's so silent at first, I wonder if the too-sweet voice is ready to give in. Or maybe it abandoned me here in the once again rising stench of rot from the sweating stone walls.

"*You need only pass through the door. You MUSSSSSSTTTTT before*—" The hiss of the too-sweet voice warbles and disappears, replaced by the slithering voice.

"*You are nothing. You are nothing. You are nothing,*" it repeats as if whispered from inside my skull.

The hairs on my neck stand on end as I scowl and step forward to inspect the identical doors.

How do I select the right door? I think, but then a horrible stench swells to fill the room. A stench like the air has not left this room in centuries. It smells like fevers and raw sewage until the air is not fit to breathe. Breath leaves my lungs as my vision narrows in the toxic cloud of the room.

In a panic, I use my fading strength to pull the closest door open and step through.

"Violet where are—"

I hear Dirge's voice so clearly. I whip around just as the door shuts behind me, and all that is left behind is stone.

"DIRGE! MOSS! GOURD!" I hammer my fists against the stone. "ZAY, SOMEBODY!"

And somebody does answer, but it's the too-sweet voice. The sugared tone caresses my ear, making me shiver.

"*Wrong door, you'll need to be faster.*"

I wheel around, knife in hand, cutting at the air in a blazing silver arc. "SHOW YOURSELF! ENOUGH GAMES!"

"Do you not miss the scent of the sea? Your freedom is just on the other side of this door. You only have to choose it."

"I heard Dirge's voice; they're not at the water!" I shout.

Yet again, I'm where I started in the same chamber with the identical doors. But the three doors have become eight. "This trick is getting really old."

"Child, child," the sugary voice demurs, *"I did not tell you to choose the door of lies. That was your own free choice, was it not?"*

"You also never mentioned there *was* a door of lies." I cross my arms skeptically.

The slithering voice begins a chorus of *"Forget your name. Forget your name. Forget your name."* It multiplies now, and beneath its whisper is a long, tortured groan. My ears grow hot, and a sharp pain stabs my temples. It's as if the growing voices have weight that presses down, down, down on my skull from all sides. I hurl myself at the third door on the left, smashing through its hinges and feeling its weight buckle beneath my feet.

"Reveal yourself! In the name of the Heaven of Hori—" It's Gourd's voice, clipped and unmistakable this time, then gone as soon as the door I passed through slams behind me.

A frustrated scream burns in my throat as I find myself in the same room. But now I count sixteen doors.

No, twenty. I blink, and they multiply.

Wrong again, forty-eight.

Forty-eight doors, sixteen each on three slowly rotating walls.

Despair floods my mind. This trap can go on forever. I can keep running through this fortress with one door out of reach until one day this putrid stench finally chokes me. My crew is behind one of these doors—my family.

"Forget your name. Forget your name. Forget your name."

I clench my jaw so hard I fear I may crack my teeth.

"You are owned. You are owned. You are mine."

"So we're just doing all the classics tonight, huh?" I bite my lip in frustration.

"My kingdom was born of your filth."

The slithering voice vibrates inside my head as dark presses against the weary torches lighting the room.

"Trust nothing, drowned child, trust nothing but—"

"*Me,*" the sugary voice cuts in, almost singing.

I massage my temples and study the movement of the doors.

Think Violet, think. I need to look at this from a different angle. I'm only one person facing forty-eight doors. If all the doors are lies, then how am I ever going to find the rest of my crew, let alone my dad? If only I could somehow open each door at once . . .

Inspiration strikes like cold rain, forcing me to my feet.

"Are you ready to answer, child?" the sugary voice croons.

"I am," I proclaim.

I sit on the filthy ground and cross my legs, clearing my throat as the light dies around me. I pick up clumps of sand from the ground and grip them tight.

"Wind, I would like to tell you a story of the continent of the sun," I begin, and feel the air stir around me in answer.

A broad smile crosses my face as the flames of the torches rise again in curiosity.

"*You are nothi*—" the slithering voice begins, but I raise my voice and shove it away.

"There once was a palace at the edge of the world, where all the doors sang lies," I continue.

"*Drowned child, cease this. Your friends will die if you*—" the sugary voice insists as the rotating walls slow their spinning.

"There were too many doors to count," I continue, feeling the wind bend to listen as it takes the sand from my palms, giving shape to figures the same size and shape as me.

"*Forget your name. Forget your name. Forget*—"

"But a captain called Violet for the color of the sky at her birth would not surrender her name, for she knew the secret of the Fortress of the Singing Door, the history it wanted her to forget."

"*CEASE THIS! THERE IS NO SECRET! THERE IS NO SECRET!*"

The sugary and slithering voices braid together in a vicious harmony, rattling the doors.

But I do not flinch, because the captain of the *Chainbreaker* does not flinch.

I finish my story and see my wind clones, all forty-seven of them, each positioned in front of a different door. I stand before the forty-eighth, knife in hand.

"Every door in a castle of slaves sings the same lie"—I draw my arm back and feel the point of my knife sink into the waterlogged wood—"that there was truly only one door all along."

As one, my clones and I stab forty-eight knives into the doors.

The fortress squeals in agony, the slithery and sugared voices bubbling as the walls of the fortress melt away like candle wax. The light of the false sun returns, and I hear water rushing away from me.

I open my eyes and see my crew, spluttering water from their lungs, splayed on the floor of the obsidian cave. Everyone except for Moss, who points behind me wordlessly. The waters of the first mask at the entrance drain away into the pit that makes up the Depths.

Two more to go.

And then the tolling of a bell rings the walls as a great cry goes up.

"Well"—Dirge spits the last of the water from her lungs as the alarm builds—"there goes the element of surprise."

— 31 —

"RUN! Get back to the bridge!" I bellow.

"Which one?" Dirge asks, pointing to the forked path where there are two bridges—one leading up and back to the mouth of the cave where we entered, and the other leading deeper into the Depths.

But it's too late. Pointer guards spill over one another down the narrow bridge we ran across to enter the chamber we are standing in now. The shark-demons run toward us from the top of the central spire, mouths foaming with hunger. The bridge sags under the weight of the screeching shark-demons.

If we don't get back out of the mouth of the chamber, the bottleneck of enemy soldiers will be on us in seconds.

The crew doesn't hesitate as we sprint to the entrance of the cave where the first screaming mouth has evaporated. We pass through the mouth of the chamber and onto the small platform of igneous rock.

"I've never seen this many of them before," Zay rasps, eyes wild as he scans the enemies advancing along the rickety bridge toward us, blocking our only way back to the ship.

Dirge fixes a bolt to her crossbow and fires a Stormbolt into the first wave of Pointers. The storm spell explodes between the advancing shark-demons as ten, twelve, fifteen are flung into the air and disappear below with a splash.

Gourd smacks down Dirge's crossbow arm as she prepares another volley. Dirge growls and wheels to face her as another wave of the enemy soldiers scrambles over their dissolving friends with hunger etched in every line of their shark faces.

"What'd you do that for?" Dirge demands.

"So you wouldn't take out the bridge that's our only way back out once we have the taken Reapers," Gourd shoots back before pointing to a bridge that leads down into the unlit dark.

"But we don't know what's down there. We can't afford to have the enemy at our back, either," Dirge hisses in response.

But there's no time to debate because the second wave of Pointers is upon us. Unfortunately for the Children of the Shark, though, Zay is all over them. All eleven years of Crest's genius shipbuilder spins into the battle like a tornado, dropping one Pointer soldier with an axe buried where its heart would have been before pivoting and slicing at another. Zay's hair beads flash steel as Dirge fires a second Stormbolt that sends ripples over the bridge, the ropes creaking ominously.

I whip my head between the two paths; the left one is

unoccupied and would take us deeper into enemy territory, while the way back to the *Moony* is . . . well, covered with a whole river of the enemy.

"We have no choice. Follow me!" I call out, beckoning everyone down the bridge to our left, farther into the pit, and toward the second mask of rushing water.

"How do we know we'll be okay down there?" Zay asks, silver teeth gleaming as he yanks an axe from another demon and dodges an attack.

I feel a rush of anger fly through me as one of Zay's braids is cut by the claw of the Pointer and flies over the edge of the bridge. I channel a storm around a bolt of my own and fire it above the heads of the enemy, sheets of rain coming down as lightning threatens above.

"We don't," Gourd concedes.

Dirge's mouth forms a slash as, with a wet screech, the last of the second Pointer wave falls by Zay's blade.

"Damn, Zay is in the lead now." She kicks a rock.

"Do you think this is a game?!" Gourd asks, dumbstruck.

"No, but making a game of it does help alleviate the feeling of certain doom. And I'm a better shot when I don't feel like I'm about to die."

"Fair enough."

We ease our way around the central column of the Depths, but the Children of the Shark begin to leap from the bridge above, trying to reach ours below. Most miss, but a few land on the groaning bridge, fangs bared.

Gourd calls for a burst of wind that knocks six of the Pointers screaming into the distance, but it also sets the rope bridge swaying with a few ominous pops. I shoot a quick look up and curse; there are at least sixty more Pointers judging the distance between their bridge and ours. The demonic sharks' muscles shine like pearls in the eerie light as four more leap forward. Without a word, Dirge and I each aim a bolt and find our mark as the Pointers hiss and melt in the air. But as Zay and Gourd hold the line against the Pointers ahead of us, more are starting to spill down from where we came.

We cannot afford to be trapped.

Meanwhile, more Pointers begin to judge the distance accurately on the rope bridge ahead of us, and while they don't weigh much, the bridge could snap at any moment.

"We have to keep going! Move, move, move!" I holler, summoning my wind-knives and hurling three with deadly accuracy to slow the surge of Pointers behind us.

I charge forward and find Zay is in step with me. Dirge's Stormbolt blows a squad of the enemy out of the air above us. I aim to fire a bolt into the chest of one, but before I can, another has swung a rusted sword that misses my face by inches but cracks the crossbow, sending it spinning off my gauntlet into the dark pit below. I growl, flicking my knife to my hand and cut through the enemy.

We dodge and slice our way across until we are all standing before the second mask of agonized water.

Well, almost all of us.

Gourd's the last to cross the bridge, but her eyes are on the largest Pointer I have ever seen. Its broad face pulls the corners of its fanged mouth into a crooked smile as it bounces along the rope bridge to cheers from its friends. It can't be, not the Great White Pointer. Not the same demon that killed Mom. I knew I had rotten luck, but this?!

"Gourd." I beckon.

"I say we take out the bridge; it's the only way," Dirge says, lining up her shot.

But Gourd slowly lowers Dirge's crossbow with her hand. "No, this one's mine."

"No, it's not! We have to all go through the mouth," I insist, pulling at Gourd's shoulder, but her gaze is far away.

"Someone needs to make sure that monstrosity doesn't follow us."

The Great White Pointer has stopped running and is now sauntering like a gladiator along the bridge as the other Pointers chomp their jaws together in rhythm.

"We can deal with it once we're inside. I can't lose you. Not like this. Gourd, please, get inside the cave. That's an order," I plead, tears pricking the corners of my eyes. "I won't lose you, I won't."

Gourd smiles sadly at me. "You're right, you won't," she says softly.

And just like that, an immense wave of wind forms

around her palm, and my eyes widen as Gourd sends me, Zay, Dirge, and Moss through the watery mask. The last thing I see before the nausea of passing through the water forces my eyes shut is Gourd, wiry muscles tensed as she punches another fang from the Great White's hungry smile.

← 32 →

When my eyes open, it's so dark they may as well be shut. Thin slats of light struggle through from above our heads and beneath our feet. I can feel the buck and sway of the tides below.

"Hey, is anyone else still here?" I ask tremulously.

Dirge grunts in response as a miniature storm flares around her hand, lighting the space between us and throwing long shadows over Moss's face as he nods.

But Zay is missing.

My stomach feels hollowed out as I look around for the best shipbuilder in the Five Heavens, but his wide, excited smile is nowhere near. Instead, out ahead I see a long stretch of wood like the hull of a ship, but the boards are warped—and shifting. Walls start to rotate and form new corridors until it looks like a kind of puzzle box.

"Ugh, not more of these mazes . . ." Dirge groans, her lightning growing brighter with her frustration.

"So you also saw the castle then?" I ask. I stare back at the space we just came from and strain my ears for the sounds of battle, of Gourd, of anything. But there's only the sound of the shifting maze ahead of us.

"Yeah." Dirge grimaces.

"You guys saw something?" Moss asks, chin tilted up.

Both of us pause a moment to stare at Moss as the floor of the maze jolts beneath us.

"Did you not, Moss?" I ask calmly.

Moss is about to answer when I feel the wood beneath our feet spin. The stench of rotting wood smacks me full in the face as the clatter of the boards swallows our shouts. Dirge grabs my hand and I snatch Moss's wrist and cling for dear life as the Hull Maze swallows us.

A guttural moan rolls down the length of the ship while we get back on our feet to look around.

"It wants us to play," Moss says gravely, his voice a whisper almost lost in the sound of clattering wood.

Dirge rolls her eyes and is definitely about to say something rude, when I hear a whistle, a note, and then another. It's an old song, "The Ballad of Moon and Shore." It's a song from Horizon, a song that has two parts, one meant for the morning, and the other to be sung hours later at night. I perk my ears up.

"Gourd?!"

The sound of the shifting walls clatters to a halt as no response comes for a beat, then a whistle with the melody of the second half of the ballad arrives. It's a sad song, but it was one of my dad's favorites. It's a duet about two Passengers, brothers, who were separated during the Storm at the Edge of the World. They wandered the tides and all the Five Heavens in search of each other for years with one singing to the shoreline and the other humming to the moon until their music brought the brothers back to each other at last.

"Dad?" I ask, remembering him humming the song as we blew the steam off spoonfuls of black-eyed peas.

I step forward into a corridor and toward the sound, Moss and Dirge following close behind as I signal for quiet.

"Zay? Is that you? Whistle the moon's theme if it's you!"

Zay's whistle comes again moments before the sound of nails ripped from their moorings signals the walls re-forming into a dead end behind us. Dirge and I share a look of relief at knowing Zay is somewhere in the maze.

"I hate puzzles. Like, I get not wanting to give away his position in case there are Pointers . . . or worse, somewhere in here." Dirge spits, the wet sound echoing.

"I . . . definitely am not a fan of this puzzle, but at least it seems like we're making progress," I say.

The moon's melody comes from a corner to the far right as the wood settles into place. We all dash through the temporarily still wood.

Down to a crew of four. I grimace. *I have to fix this. I have to find the way out.*

Zay whistles the moon's theme again as the walls rumble

into motion, contorting and shifting the hallways again until it looks like everything is a dead end.

"Hey, Vi, how does Zay know the pattern when the walls are going to shift, but we don't?" Moss says, tapping his chin near me.

I stop in my tracks. I've been so busy just trying to get to Zay, I hadn't asked how he knew to find us. And what—or who—is stopping him from just speaking aloud?

I give Dirge a signal to halt, remembering an old Tide-watcher proverb.

Where there's seawater, there's sight.

That was why Zay chose this song specifically, to tell us to Tidewatch the water at our feet and find our way back to each other. He really is a prodigy after all, getting his whole plan across to us without speaking one word the enemy could hear. I plunge my hand into the murky waters at our feet and feel a wave of nausea pass through me, but I grit my teeth and press farther until I am touching the bottom of the boat.

"Violet, you don't know what's in that water. That's disgusting!" Dirge retches, choking on the air.

"Hold on, Dirge. Violet's got the squishy look on her face that means she's figured something out!" Moss says, earning a snort-laugh from Dirge.

I'd glare at the two of them, but my eyes are closed, searching for some proof of my theory. The waters are cloudy and stink of stomach acid, salt, and rusted metal. Waters that I can read as a Tidewatcher, waters that the wood of the Hull Maze's shifting walls has drunk in. I feel the Tide-watcher magic catch along my fingers just as Zay whistles out the moon's theme again. My theory was right—I can see the water in the wood of the walls. Through my Tide-watcher vision, the wood of the shifting Hull Maze glimmers a faint sickly green, so different from the suffocating darkness around us—polluted, but alive with magic. I press my mind out farther into the water, willing the nausea away.

"C'mon, Zay, where are you—" I mumble to myself.

I don't finish as I feel my own stomach acid churn in response, and I vomit into the waters. Acid rips fire up my throat as I cough and sputter.

"Knew something wasn't right with this water." Dirge groans. "Violet, we won't find Zay this way."

"Well, what other option is there?" I say, voice distant as I try to screw my eyes tighter and ignore the empty feeling in my stomach.

Have to remember the walls were left, right, forward, forward. Or no, it's forward, left, left, right! No, that's—

Dirge's hand is a warm weight on my shoulder as she calls me back in. "The maze doesn't want us to win, Vi."

I blink at the nickname; it's simple, but only Moss ever calls me that. *Only my friends ever call me that.*

Dirge continues, "We have a saying in Shard: *A time for words, and a time for fire always sit beneath the same moon.*"

"I thought you said you hated puzzles?" Moss quips, face bunched and still staring at himself in the filthy water.

"Puzzles and proverbs aren't the same thing, but basically it means that there's a time for thinking, but there's also a time for burning things down. This maze wants us to keep thinking inside it forever, trying to find our way through. But we only got out of the first chamber because you, Violet, stabbed the door."

"So what? We just try and tear it down? We're going to call a storm in the middle of this maze?"

I feel a pang of guilt thinking of Sunshower. How he'd be here if I hadn't let anger cloud my judgment. If I had just thought more. If I had just been better.

"Beats staying here, wandering forever in this torture juice," Dirge concludes.

She brings the storm in her hand down to clasp mine. The clouds tickle my knuckles as they expand, and I feel our powers flowing together. Lightning crackles along my palm.

Rage needs a home just like anything else, I think, power feeding on the pit of rage in my chest.

"What about Zay?" I ask, electricity surging through my body.

"Maybe we should just ask him, since I think any enemies in here are going to hear us smashing the ship from the inside?" Moss shrugs then follows up at the top of his lungs; "ZAY, DO YOU MIND IF WE JUST TRY AND BREAK THE WHOLE PRISON WITH A BIG STORM?!"

Silence follows for a beat before a familiar voice says, "Well, when you phrase it like that, how can I say no?"

I almost lose my grip on the storm swelling between us, my knees wanting to buckle and my chest inflating with laughter.

I watch the storm clouds multiply as I let my mind drift to Zay, to Moss's terrified face as the manacle flower dragged him into the first chamber, to Sunshower and how I never saw him fall into the water.

To Dad and how I did see him fall.

Lightning explodes at all angles just as the walls of the Hull Maze begin to shift to form new prisons. But instead, the lightning fractures them to matchsticks. The sound of splintering wood fills my ears along with a roar, Dirge's and my powers amplify each other.

Our storm devours the hull. Nails and boards rip apart and crash into the water. With a flash and scream of lightning, the prison shatters around us, and the world goes bright white to the point I have to shut my eyes. Everything rushes away with the gurgle of foul water spilling out and away from us as the second mask shatters.

Dirge and Moss and I and, yes, a bloody-lipped Zay all cough on the ground as the second mask's chamber drains of water. The water flows away from us, rushing behind and out into the Depths. I signal a thumbs-up to Zay, who grins weakly before pushing himself to his feet with the handle of one of his axes.

"Nicely done, you four," comes Gourd's familiar voice.

I wheel to see Gourd leaning in the doorway, a long gash running across her forehead and one eye nearly eclipsed by a bruise, but alive. Despite myself, I grin back.

And then, behind her, the entire pit begins to scream.

— 33 —

The Shriek begins as a humming in the stone. The bridge that leads down into the pit to the third and final mask of rushing water begins to rumble with the force of the Shriek. It builds, crawling through the marrow of my bones and threatening to crack my jaw. I slam my hands over my ears, but whatever is in the pit, its scream won't be denied. I look into the pit again and see two things:

1. The Shriek has built into a gale, a tornado of roiling loud air that carries discarded weapons and rusted leaves up with vicious force.

2. A long line of Pointer soldiers slowly maneuvers over the violently swaying bridges, hunger in every line of their twisted faces.

I try to bark an order, but the screaming is everywhere now, and I can barely string two thoughts together. Every story I can tell the wind is stolen in the noise.

Think, Violet, think. I press my hands against my eyes, trying to relieve the pressure, then immediately clap my hands back over my ears as the Pointer soldiers continue to advance across the bridge.

The pressure builds again behind my eyes as I squeeze them, wishing I could form a bubble around myself, just a moment's peace, just a—

Realization spreads electric over my whole face as I take a deep breath and prepare for the hot pain of uncovering my ears again. I cup my hands and whisper into my palms, "Preserve us," and I feel the wind form a bubble of air around me. I drag myself over to Gourd, who marvels at the small bubble of swirling air in my palm. As she takes my palms in hers, I watch the bubble grow and grow until it envelops the whole crew. The Shriek still rattles up from the ground, but at long last, we can hear each other again. Gourd maintains the bubble of wind around us by keeping up my chant.

Zay walks up and lightly punches my shoulder. "You never cease to amaze, do you, Violet Chainbreaker?" Zay grins, then pulls me into a rib-cracking hug before holding me at arm's length and giving me a silvery smile.

"Not to be a downer, but we do need to get moving soon, no?" Dirge side-eyes the hug, and we part with a blush prickling beneath my cheeks.

"I don't know how many Pointers Gourd took out—"

"Enough that they were regrouping before you four re-emerged." Gourd grunts, touching her bruised eye with a smile.

"Well, thanks for that." Dirge muses, "We are definitely getting closer. While the rest of us were inside that maze, I thought I could feel something. But now that the second mask has shattered and we're lower in the chamber, I can feel them."

"Them?" I ask, trying not to let myself hope.

"The captured Reapers. It's like the more we undo these chambers, the less cloudy everything else here is." Dirge's finger traces her wing tattoo. "There's still horrors here I can't see clearly, but there are hearts beating down there."

A brief quiet steals over the group as the gravity of what Dirge said sinks in. Well, as quiet as it can get with the chamber beyond screaming bloody murder. But beneath that scream, at the bottom of the Depths, Dad is waiting.

"Then we cannot fail. We need to move before the Pointers start making their way back down. Good job back there, with the maze." I offer a fist bump to Dirge.

"I think, given the strength of the wind from the Shriek, we have a beat to come up with a plan. And you're welcome on the maze. For the record: Breaking things is almost *always* my pleasure," she responds, adjusting her nose ring slightly before doing a little bow.

Zay and I exchange a brief side-eye before the excitable

inventor's full cheeks split into a grin. "Okay, so I've finished my calculations and—"

"When did you start?" Moss asks, which, honestly is a fair question.

"Calculations of what?" Dirge and I ask simultaneously.

"How we're going to make it across. And luckily, it's the same way we got in. We'll make a windbubble. If we take turns maintaining the windbubble two Windthreaders at a time, the magic should have enough counter-velocity that the Shriek won't carry us up so fast we get smashed on the ceiling like overripe mangos."

"I could kiss your brain right now." Dirge smirks.

"Oh, please don't. I like it inside my head and want to keep it kiss-free, thank you!" Zay smiles at his own joke, and only Moss joins him.

"And you're sure this will work?" I ask.

"Well, you can never be exactly sure of anything with magic . . ." Zay strokes his chin as the first Pointer to set foot on the bridge nearest us releases its grip and is yanked upward by the Shriek.

"Okay, follow-up, then," Dirge says, pointing to the flying shark-demon. "Would the bubble be able to prevent us from being tossed around like sacks of rice? Because we're not getting across that bridge otherwise."

The Shriek somehow swells to a greater volume as a chunk of black rock cracks from the central pillar, but Zay is all smiles as he pushes his iron-rimmed glasses back up his nose.

"Oh that? That, I'm positive of."

The trip across the bridges is perilous and slow, the Shriek's unrelenting howl threatening at any moment to snatch us away. We rotate Windthreading as chanting "Preserve us" begins to ring in our bones, a golden warm feeling that washes the cold from my skin. Moss shuffles along inside the ring created by me, Dirge, Zay, and Gourd. I feel the speed of the wind bring tears to my eyes and wipe them away before anyone can see.

A leaping Pointer soldier dives like an arrow from above and lands for only a second on our bubble of protection before a look of understanding dawns in its milky eyes. The soldier spins like a top and is flung bodily into the mouth of the third mask.

I expect the Pointer to disappear, to turn to smoke, or even to be swallowed by the mouth as we were the last two times. But instead, it squeals in panic, fangs flashing in the muted light as the shark's face melts away and leaves the broad face of a man in its place. A human man, he stares bemused at his own scarred hands and then up at us advancing toward him. He mouths a word, just one, which is lost in the Shriek of the Depths before his body turns to translucent gray like sickly water.

Dirge, Zay, and I wear identical expressions of confusion, fear, and pity, our jaws hanging open. We shuffle the remaining distance and pause before the endlessly agonized mouth of the third mask.

Cold dread sits in every muscle of my body. I stare at the mask, and the mask stares back at me, unblinking.

"We have no choice," I finally say, turning to face the group, then addressing Dirge.

"We're close," Moss says, and everyone's eyes turn to him.

"How are you so certain?" Dirge asks, head cocked to the side.

"I told you, I can—" Moss begins, but the Shriek sends another chunk of rock from above that shatters inches from us in a cloud of dust.

I look up at the group, every set of eyes trained on me and determined, despite everything.

We're coming, Dad.

The windbubble bursts as we finish passing through the mouth of the third mask. And for once, we are all here— together. The warmth of the sun comes down, golden over the graying sands of a beach licked by a tide of gray water. In the distance, rust-colored trees sway and clink against one another. The tarnished trees almost look like they're sobbing.

I hear the sound of rushing water and realize how much I have missed it. I'm about to take my first step onto the beach, when a pang rolls through my body. It's the same nausea I felt Tidewatching in the second chamber. I recoil and look where I was about to step. A moan of disgust comes from the group as I see a horror-struck face emerging from the gray muck, mouth open and screaming without ever making a sound.

Slavetide.

— 34 —

I can't stop staring at the tortured face.

"It's just so . . . gross." Dirge curls her lip, revolted by the way it seems to be looking directly at her.

"The face?" I ask.

"Nah, all of it." Dirge gestures broadly at the beach.

"Yeah, I gotta agree; I draw the line at carnivorous beaches." Zay waves his arms at the face, trying to get its attention.

The sun begins to set, and the face finally disappears as Dirge and I venture out onto the beach to find some wood to test a theory. When we find it, a thick log as tall as both of us put together, we lower it gingerly into the water and watch the Slavetide devour it whole.

"Yup, that just about confirms it." Dirge sucks her teeth, dusting off her hands.

"I'm guessing you have a theory to explain all this mess?" I say.

"Theory? You make me sound like that egghead crush of yours." Dirge smirks as heat prickles over my face.

"Shut up! I do not!"

"Mm-hmm, the sweet taste of denial; you really miss out on that when you're hiding on your mango farm."

"Dirge," I say, "I'm assuming you wanted to show me something besides your sense of humor."

"Oh yeah, my bad, I was thinking about mangos. They really are amazing. Anyway, my theory is there's bound to be some Slavetide in the roots of these trees, and if we Tidewatch this space together, I think we can navigate without running into any more of those faces popping up out of the ground. We just have to navigate away from the nausea. I don't think they have teeth, but I also don't want to find out." Dirge makes a biting motion with her hands.

"We can share the nausea? It was overwhelming back on the tides. I felt so sick I could barely see. Are you sure this will work?" I ask, staring at my palm curiously.

"Magic amplification, truly my favorite gift from the gods of the old world and the new—the more of us there are casting one spell, the stronger we are." Dirge sticks out her palm, the setting sun painting her wing tattoo gold.

"So, you in?"

I grab her hand and immediately regret it as we plunge our hands into the soil. Unlike Tidewatching the seas between the Five Heavens where everything's open and alive with light, a blunt wave of nausea rolls through my body, and I almost lose my lunch for a second time that day. On top of that, the mud is thick, but it tells a story about the curses of the Chainmakers.

"The trees aren't trees at all." I gasp.

The "trees" are actually made of bundles of rusted chains, just like the ones that cling to the sides of the main chamber outside. Just like the manacled flower that snatched Moss by the ankle and dragged him into the first chamber. These Manacle Trees are another prison for the Chainmakers.

It's a cycle: When the sun is high in the sky and the tide rolls freely into the soil, the souls trapped in the Slavetide are drunk up like water through the roots of the Manacle Trees. The Slavetide brings the metal to life so it can grab Passengers. Then later, as the moon rises, the Slavetide drains back out from the trees and returns to the shore. The Pointers then scoop it into those massive stone jars to deploy as weapons of war.

A thought itches the edge of my brain as I grit through more nausea. Finally, I have to pull my hand away, Dirge and I both fighting off dry heaves.

I wipe my hand across my mouth. "Okay, so the good news is that I have a plan!"

"Hasn't anyone ever told you to lead with the bad news?" Dirge smiles thinly, still spluttering.

"Well, yes," I concede, "but you're not gonna like it."

"How do you know that?"

I push myself to my feet and head back toward Moss,

Zay, and Gourd, calling back over my shoulder. "Because I don't like it, either!"

When we regroup outside the forest, my prediction proves right. Nobody likes this plan, but also nobody has a better one.

So here we are, trekking under the swaying rust of the trees. My theory is right: We can trace the small amounts of water in the chains to a gateway out on the other side of the forest. From there, I predict we can get down to the bottom of the pit outside this chamber, where the captured Reapers will hopefully be. The only downside? Having to navigate our way through the muddy, horrified faces of the trapped souls of the Chainmakers. Moss's face is troubled, so I squeeze his shoulder reassuringly, and he falls in step beside me.

"Moss, can I ask you something?"

"Of course." He nods.

"Well, when I was in the first chamber coming to find you, I saw this big castle, and there were these doors that lied and—"

"Mm-hmm, Zay mentioned that when we were at the Slavetide basin."

"Okay, so that's my thing. All of us saw the castle except—"

"Me," Moss says flatly, taking a long hop-step over a gasping face in the sand.

"So, what did you see?"

Moss's face is all shadows, his eyes downcast as the wind stirs and the trees clink ominously above us.

"Nothing."

"Moss, brother, you can tell me anything. Even if it was bad."

"No," Moss clarifies, a small warble in his voice. "I mean, I saw nothing. Inky darkness in every direction. And then there were these whispers. It felt like they crept along my skin and . . ." Moss shivers.

"Oh my," I say, trying—and failing—to think of something comforting to say.

"It's okay, you saved me before they could say much." He pauses.

"What were they saying, Moss?"

The little Passenger, my boy of smoked glass, looks up into the rattling branches of the Manacle Trees.

Finally, he answers.

"Help us."

I want to ask Moss more about that inky dark and where he thinks those voices came from. I want to ask why only a Passenger could hear those voices but not see the creepy talking castle the rest of us did. I want to ask if he's okay.

But I can't because my foot has been trapped in the toothless mouth of a muddy Chainmaker, and now I'm sinking as the Manacle Trees rattle to life and attack.

"VIOLET!" Gourd, Dirge, and Zay cry in unison as I yelp and sink farther.

Within seconds, the Manacle Trees try to snatch at the crew's arms, ankles, throats—anything the chains can reach and grab.

I punch at the suckling mouth around my ankle, Moss pulling at my shoulders with all his might, but his stick-thin arms are too weak. A chain drops from the rusted tree looming over us. I punch it away in desperation, the manacle lolling open like a snake's jaw. Pain lances down my arm from striking its metal face. The manacle explodes toward me, and I duck in time, but now Moss gets captured. The writhing manacle takes the Passenger boy by the throat, holding him in the sky as he hammers translucent fists against it. Rage floods my gut, and I summon my wind around my fist to shove deep into the mouth of the muddy Chainmaker soul.

"LET. HIM. GO," I growl, punching the ground near my trapped foot, the wind around my hand spinning so fast that the face blends into the muck. When I pull my hand back, the skin is blistered and sore like I punched something hot.

I grimace and force myself up. Most of the hanging vines are attacking Gourd, Dirge, and Zay, who are struggling to fend off wave after wave of attacks. Zay's twin axes are a blur before him, while Gourd and Dirge work their Windthreader magic to twist and misdirect some of the attacking fetters before slicing them clean. In a circle around them, sixty cuffs lie in the soil like they've beheaded a whole pit of snakes.

But not the one that still holds Moss in the air. I send

a wind-knife spinning through it, shattering the chain and diving to catch Moss before he hits the ground.

"Thanks, Vi!" Moss groans, massaging his throat while we run to help the others.

God, I hope Dirge taught me how to do this well enough, I pray, lining up a shot with my crossbow and channeling the rage to the tip of the bolt. I bite my lip, exhaling as I fire and watch the rain, thunder, and lightning explode into the remaining Manacle Trees. The ground quakes as the Manacle Trees shudder and scream, their twisting limbs shattering. It sounds like an avalanche of coins landing around Zay, Dirge, and Gourd.

There's no time for words, though. Only time to run, as more living Manacles pour down from above us like a curse.

No, not like *a curse,* I think, huffing as I slice with the wind-blades in my gloves, causing my bones to vibrate. *An actual curse. A curse of the old gods and new. The gods cursed the Chainmakers to drown like this forever.*

On the other side of the forest, an ornate stone entryway leads out to a cliff. Rust squeals above us as we head toward it at a dead sprint. Moss is huffing, mouth lolling and eyes wide with terror and exhaustion, but he's at my side, nonetheless. I summon some of my wind and urge it to push Moss forward and into Gourd's waiting arms, as I'm about to be the last out.

I load another bolt into my crossbow, ready to fire the second I make it to the edge of the cliff. A wild plan forms in my head. I let the rage of losing Sunshower, Dad, Mom, and who knows how many others to the curses and appetites of the Chainmakers course through my fingers—becoming a small storm that I fix to the end of the crossbow's bolt. I leap over a final face in the muck and feel my foot hit firm stone for the first time in hours.

Now across the entryway, I roll forward, wheel, and stare into the brightly lit prison. The hunger is endless, even in death. I exhale and shoot a Stormbolt that slams into the stone archway, causing it to collapse toward the Slavetide on the heads of writhing shackles that were giving chase. The boom of collapsing rock echoes all through the Depths as I cough away the slag dust.

Gourd's forehead is bleeding, her gaze flitting between me and Moss as she tries to figure if either of us is hurt. Or maybe she's deciding which of us to lecture about the danger of setting off an exploding weapon right above the cliff we're standing on. Zay nurses a bruise on his left cheek while Dirge gives me a very slow clap.

"I knew it was a good idea to teach you that move."

I smile exhaustedly, breath still sharp and hot in my lungs. I kneel to look at the dented and crushed metal of the manacles, finally lying still like dead snakes in the rubble. Beyond the edge of the cliff is the very bottom of the Depths. I pull myself to my feet and kick the severed, lifeless chains over the edge of the cliff. I can't help but laugh.

Hundreds of years ago, the gods cursed the Chainmakers to drown, and now I've buried them.

— 35 —

Dirge holds a miniature storm in her free palm, and the lightning illuminates the strange bottom of the pit.

From above, it looks like the largest bowl I've ever seen. The gray stone is worn unnaturally smooth. Water that made up the third chamber's entrance streams into the bowl, swirling in a small vortex before draining away into the perfect circular hole in the center.

Down below, will we find Dad, Sunshower, and the other captive Reapers?

"That's not ominous at all . . ." Zay says, flicking a bead of sweat from his brow.

"Where do you think it goes?" Dirge adds, eyes scanning.

No one answers, quiet ruling for a stretch of moments.

And how are we supposed to get down there?

Dirge finally breaks the contemplative silence. "So, I'm guessing we have to follow the demon-water, right?"

Instead of answering that question, Moss asks the other

one that everyone is thinking. "Even if we can find our way down there, how would we get back up?"

A shudder passes through me like a shock of cold rain. Beneath that hole is maybe Dad, but also maybe a fourth chamber that might be harder to escape from than the previous three combined.

Gourd looks like she's wishing she had an infinite length of rope. Or a ladder. A ladder would also be nice.

I scan the edges of the bowl, trying to determine if this is another puzzle or a last line of defense. A single clue would be helpful.

"I think we should just jump," Dirge finally declares, shaking me out of my thoughts.

Gourd side-eyes. "And if we don't make it?"

"Then we'll be as doomed as we are now at the bottom of a trench in the ocean packed to the gills with enemies that want to kill us. But we can't just keep staring at it like it's gonna magically get closer."

"Well, maybe that's what *you* were doing." Gourd scoffs. "Some of us were assessing the situation, looking for clues, taking literally any moment of this mission seriously."

"I make jokes, you make stress headaches. We all have our roles to play, but it doesn't change things."

"We did not come all this way to fling ourselves off a cliff when we are so close. You need to pause, you need to think, you—"

"Enough," I finally growl, standing between them. "You

two really could be related. The arguing needs to stop so we can plan."

"Vi, there's no outsmarting this." Dirge gestures at the vast canyon between us and the bowl.

The darkness around the gray stone bowl is so absolute it almost hurts my eyes.

Why couldn't I have been born with wings? I sigh.

I look around the group, noticing everyone's shoulders are sagging. Zay inspects an axe and runs a small whetstone along it. In the dark, the noise rebounds to us and it sounds like an army is sharpening their knives above us.

Which, I guess they are.

"Zay." I clear my throat and stare at the inventor, cocking an eyebrow. "What are the calculations on using Windthreading for flying?"

"Um, you add *nope* to *don't even think about it,* and then you carry the *no, seriously, this is a terrible idea.*" Zay deadpans, pausing for a laugh that never comes. "But, in all seriousness . . . it doesn't work. Why do you ask? And why are you still smiling? Oh, this is going to be the scariest part yet, isn't it?"

"Looking back on it," Zay says, arms splayed out to his sides as he contemplates the jump, "maybe I could have been clearer about how this has *never* worked before."

"Neither did missions to the Depths for the past hundreds

of years!" Dirge chimes in, a little too encouraging from someone who doesn't have to go first.

Zay squints in annoyance at Dirge and looks back to me. "All right, explain to me again what you're trying to do?"

"Well, the Pointers' architects didn't give us stairs, but I think we can build our own!" I point to Gourd, Dirge, and myself. "You're definitely right that we won't be able to fly, but what if the wind just cushioned us every step down? Like, we make little platforms and hop between them. Then once you're down there, you'll be able to use your Windthreader magic to do the same thing! We just keep going until we're all on the other side."

"Like skipping a stone over water!" Moss claps.

Zay nods nervously. I take his hand and squeeze it.

Zay stops trembling for the moment, and I watch his broad shoulders rise and fall as his belly fills with air and releases. He turns and gives me a signature grin, his silver fangs shining in the dark like blades. "All right, I will go first, *but* when the story of this mission is told, I will need at least three very cool nicknames, like *Darkwalker* or *Silverfang* or . . ."

"I will never call you Silverfang . . . but I will laugh at three of your jokes, maybe even five."

Zay giggles as Dirge fixes me with a look that says *you'd have been better off just calling him Darkwalker.*

I shrug as Zay signals that he's ready. He walks out onto the air, followed by Gourd with Moss clinging to her neck, then Dirge. They quickly step along the pillowy air and glide down into the bowl. They beckon me to them.

When it's my turn to stand at the edge, though, the darkness looks solid and menacing.

And what about escaping even if Dad is down there?

If he's even alive, says a voice in my head.

I consider taking a step back from the edge, but another voice responds. *And who are you to come so far only to surrender?*

I cock my shoulders back. I know the answer now as I leap off the edge and feel the wind catch me just long enough to hop to the next spinning cloud of air, and the next, and the next . . . I am nearly at the end, almost in the arms of my crew, as the biggest jump approaches. I stare at the bowl, and from above, it looks like a huge gray eye. I aim for its center. I leap, wind rushing around me as I fall and let the dark claim me.

— ⬩ 36 ⬩ —

The trickle of dingy water echoes everywhere in the vast stone chamber. My frown deepens as my eyes adjust to the light. The chamber at the bottom of the Depths is . . . very boring? Compared to the complexity of the chambers that preceded it, it feels like the Children of the Shark have been fighting tooth and nail to defend a storage room.

"Um, Violet?" Zay's voice tremors, his finger pointing upward.

To my left? Smooth gray stone.

My right? Smooth gray stone.

Beneath me? You guessed it!

But above me? The three watery masks of pain that had previously guarded the three chambers we passed through to get here orbit slowly, suspended in the air, their mouths tracing words but saying nothing.

"Should we, uh, ask them a question?" I say, hoping someone else has an idea.

"Maybe this is where we put them down once and for all?" Dirge says, already fixing a bolt to her crossbow before I gently press her arm back down.

Gourd snorts and studies the faces above. When we were getting sucked through or escaping into them by the skin of our teeth, there wasn't much time to really, um, get to know your local creepy masks of water. But looking at them now, my brow furrows and a nauseous feeling creeps through my bones. What is going on? Is this another trap? We escaped the Slavetide chamber only for a giant bomb of water that might also be Slavetide to explode above our heads?

Dirge scowls up at the unspeaking faces and stalks off to do a lap of the chamber. She circles quickly, pressing the stone at weird angles before slinking back over to us.

"No secret panels in the walls." The frown lines of Dirge's face deepen as she looks at me.

I know instantly what she's implying.

They aren't here. We've come all this way for—

"Does anyone else think they look a bit like . . . us?" Moss's voice derails my thoughts.

"What?" I ask, a little sharper than I mean to.

"Wait, I think he has a point." Zay adds, pointing back up at the faces, whose mouths are even more open now.

I look again and realize these are not the faces of Chainmakers. Instead, the masks of agony have our jaws and hair, our full lips. These faces could have been Reapers, or cousins.

What in the name of the Chainbreakers is—

239

"Oh, you little *fool*! I understand now." Dirge smacks her own forehead so hard I fear she may bruise her brain.

"What is your problem?" Gourd hisses.

But Dirge ignores her. She paces, speaking in rapid-fire half sentences that none of us can make sense of.

"Deep below, a being in immense—Not living, not dead. You little fool, Whisper, it was always the pain . . . How did you not see?"

"Dirge, you're not making sense. Can you just talk to me like a person?" I move to take Dirge by the wrist but stop short as she wheels to look at me.

"Violet, the Depths are a hivemind, I don't know how I didn't put it together before, but it's powered by the souls of the Passengers. This was the thing I couldn't get the shape of before we came in. Remember at the bottom of the pit, that echo that just felt *wrong*? That unfathomable pain? And isn't it strange that there aren't any Passengers in the pit despite the fact the Pointers have been kidnapping souls for centuries? It was because they became *this*. The masks above us, the water, it's all made of tortured Passengers! Now, something is coming—I can feel it in my marrow. It's a trap, it was all a trap!"

Alarm surges through my body as I look around and see that we are, in fact, trapped with no exits. At the bottom of the ocean.

"Well, I mean, we can still make our way back to the ship, right?" Zay asks, confused and probably not used to needing magic explained to him.

As Dirge keeps pacing, ignoring us, Moss's eyes go wide with horror. "She's right, something feels us here, and it's coming, Vi! We have to get out of here *right now!*"

I'm about to reply when an earth-shattering *BOOM* consumes the bowl. The sound of rock cracking above us swallows all sound. I call my wind-knives to me, the Mark of the Scythe flaring to life on my forearm.

And that's when everything about the chamber changes.

The three masks let loose a choked warble, and a grinding noise like bone against bone fills my eardrums. With that, the great stone chamber begins to rotate, the waters part to either side of the room, then re-form each time with a wet slap.

I chance a glance at my crew, each of them battle-ready with weapons drawn and clearly waiting on my mark to fire. The waters at our ankles tremble again, slapping together even faster as they change color from a murky blue to a purple that nearly burns my eyes with its brightness.

And just as I'm about to start barking orders to retreat and strategize, a woman rises from the water. She is rail thin and muscular with the dyed white cornrows of a Reaper of Shard.

Realization begins to dawn as first one, then four, then seven Reapers rise from the waters face down. The captured seven all stare at us, their eyes blazing with a thin yellow energy that looks like pus. They stand perfectly still, barely breathing, silently aligned in a V formation before the final point in their group rises last from the water.

Half his locks are white or gray, and his beard is as tangled with saltwater as I've ever seen it. But the scar near the cheek, the half-amused smile, even now? The way he somehow is still talking with his hands, though I can't hear what he's saying for all the noise in my head.

No, says the voice in my head.

No, says another.

"Dad?" I hear my voice sputter as he nods with his terrible backlit eyes, so bright I could swear something in him is on fire.

⟵ 37 ⟶

When the captured Reapers speak, it is with one voice.
Dad's face is blank, as if he isn't truly seeing me. I fight
to keep my shoulders back and stand tall like a captain, even
as the eyes of the man who taught me everything are wreathed
in yellow energy.

"Violet Moon?" the captured eight say.

I push down a sob hearing my dad's voice lost in some
kind of horrific trap. A trap that I've strolled right into.

Still, I step forward, fists balled at my sides, not taking
my eyes off Dad. It feels like each time I blink, he may disappear all over again.

"Who are you?" I growl, finally.

The eight respond, "We are the lost ones, a choir that
sings only in whispers. At the beginning of this world, we
were who the storm left behind."

I bite my lip, trying to wrap my head around the riddle.
Was Dirge's theory correct? The souls of Passengers smashed

together into one consciousness? I try for a different question, eyes still locked on Dad.

"Are you in charge of the Depths?"

"No, we are its prisoner. As more Passengers have been taken, we have grown in size. We are a power source for the Queen Wound, the intelligence and curse that guides the Depths. We have been forced to serve the will of this curse for millennia. The Chainmakers fell to the Depths, and their curse is bound to us, drawn to the pain like moths to a light."

"So wait." Zay can't help but interrupt. "You were there when the Chainbreakers brought on the Storm at the Edge of the World?"

All the heads of the Reapers snap in Zay's direction, and he slides his hand to his axes before their eyes soften in answer.

"Some of us were there with the first ships, when the gods opened up the ocean and the Chainbreakers traveled to the Tides of the Lost. But we were left behind, the ancestors who could not be found. We fell within the curse and have been bound here ever since."

Horror sprawls across all our faces. I hear myself ask a question.

"Do you have a name?"

"We have many. The Queen Wound calls us her Gravemind. Our individual names are so knotted within it, we have forgotten them. Our pain is fuel to the Queen Wound, the Depths' hivemind. And our memories are prisons for its enemies. We are the lost ones who have become a monument to the curse's corruption."

Gourd steps to my side and asks the question on everyone's mind. "Spirits, Passengers, cousins, I am sorry for your pain. But why seize the living when before you only took Passengers?"

I stare at Dad's and Sunshower's faces, searching for any sign that Gourd registers to them, that they are still in there. But their faces are stone, monuments of men I knew but lost to the gods of loss.

A purple pulse throbs in the water, and an ache sets into my joints.

Out of the corner of my eye, I see Zay's teeth gritted and focused on a woman with close-cropped gray hair. *Zay's mom.* But is he wincing because he's feeling the sickness in the water or because his mom may never be able to say his name again?

Finally, the Gravemind responds in slow, halting phrases. "We are the monument, and we are the catalyst. The Children of the Shark draw their power and consciousness from our agony, feeding on it. But slivers of who we once were live on. Over time, we have relearned to see and sometimes briefly control the Children of the Shark. We have stolen your living to ask for your help."

"Then what are you asking us?" I stamp my foot, sending water flying out, and a sharp pain jolts through my left knee.

The Gravemind's answer is immediate, unflinching. "We

are the monument, but we have no hands with which to tear ourselves down."

"What are y'all talking about?" Dirge asks, reading my mind.

"The Queen Wound, the heart of the curse, lies below us. But we cannot release ourselves, and so we stole Reapers who might be able to help by controlling the Children of the Shark."

Fury blazes through me as finally I understand. The Gravemind, made of thousands upon thousands of abandoned and captured souls, centuries upon centuries of Passengers dating back to the very first Chainbreakers, is bound by the consequences of a curse meant only for the Chainmakers. And they are chained to the heart of another.

This is why my father was stolen, to pay the debts of the Chainbreakers.

The Gravemind's sixteen eyes are on me again. "We beg, we have never been so close to death. Release us. We ask your forgiveness for what has been done to you with our pain."

And with that, the fallen Reapers in the Gravemind sink to their knees, palms offered out to me as seawater slips through their fingers.

"Violet, we cannot know they are telling the truth," Gourd says flatly.

My mouth contorts while I consider the kneeling Gravemind. There are eight of them and five of us; even on our best day, we'd probably be at a disadvantage. If the Gravemind wanted us dead, why come up with a story at all? Wordlessly, I sink to one knee, offering my palms out.

"I am sorry for what has been done with your pain for so many years."

I chance a glance upward and feel my chest constrict as I see that each of the Gravemind's fallen has the same tears running down their face. A bearded man's crescent moon scar fills with saltwater, but he doesn't move.

"If I free you, what becomes of the Reapers you hold?"

I brace for the answer.

"They will be released back to their minds, but there is a chance the pit itself may collapse. Though the process appears to have already begun."

All attention is on me. Out of the corner of my right eye, I see Gourd, still counting potential enemies, and Zay, calculating the magic in the air, as always. To my left, Dirge is trying to grab my attention. I shoot her a look, and Dirge mouths back *Moss*.

Panic grabs me by the throat. I whirl around and search for Moss in the pulsing purple water. I finally spot him, kneeling on the floor where the pulsing light settles in the jagged shape of a scar. Moss's fingers are lit from below, an orchid's purple, as he reaches forward to touch it. I spring up from my crouched position and barrel toward Moss, my first friend, my little brother.

Moss hears the splash of my boots and yanks his hands back from the scar-shaped light.

"I could hear them, Vi. I could hear them all." He flings his arms around me, his weight insubstantial, and I press him to my chest for a long while before I put him back down. I jab a finger at the Gravemind's fallen.

"Is that who you heard when you were in the first chamber?" My hands always look so big over his bony shoulders.

Moss's chest swells, and when he speaks there's a bass in his voice I ain't heard in a long time. "We have to help them, Vi. We have to. They're—"

"Our people." My matter-of-fact voice ricochets off the walls.

I straighten and dust off my clothes to find the Gravemind's eight, including Dad, still kneeling. I walk up to the first and offer my hand, pulling up each Reaper in succession.

"I will release you. I swear it by every star in the sky."

A shudder runs through the Gravemind, and the voice lets out a long, satisfied sigh, as if they've been drowning and are finally coming up for air.

"It has been such a long time since we saw the stars," all eight voices coo.

"Prepare to become them, dearest ancestors." I reach out and rub my hand along Dad's face, making sure he's real.

I rejoin Moss and find him studying the wound in the floor as if he's doing an impression of Zay, stroking his bony chin with his long, elegant fingers. I blink, and the image of three hands clasped together and bathed in purple light is seared behind my eyes.

I offer Moss my hand as both of us feel a surge of power pass through us. Moss's rounded cheeks split into a shocked smile. Who knew? After all this time, it turns out Moss has magic all his own.

We reach out, and my hands are bathed in purple light that calls, that sings, that pulls me close until I'm not sure if it wants to hug me or drown me. I clear my throat, gathering my new story to me—one the Tides of the Lost have never heard before, because we have been too busy living it.

"Once and still, the water tore us from each other," I begin as the dust shivers in every corner and the wind leans in to listen. "May there be forgiveness for this and plenty of stars for the fallen. Once and still, a storm made a world within the world. Once and still, a scar in the light made a curse only for our darkness."

I feel the purple light sear beneath me and shut my eyes as the Queen Wound's rage sends a fever crashing through my body. But I steady as I feel Moss's consciousness flow into mine and we speak as one.

"Once and still, we made more than one Heaven because we deserve more than one—"

A rhythmic stomp from the Gravemind's fallen begins to keep time with my story while the Queen Wound thrashes beneath us. I think if it could scream, it would. I stare above as the watered masks of the Gravemind begin to shrink and the forms and souls of Passengers float up and out the exit in the ceiling.

"Once and still, the dead floated. Once and still, the dead live alongside us. Once and still, the Heaven that held us was us."

More souls scatter as our story unspools centuries of hurt, until the last of the yellowed eyes has faded from the Gravemind's fallen. Dad looks at me and Moss, and I see him about to say my name, say anything but *Hold on to this for me, Little Fish*, like he has on a loop in my dreams for days.

But there's no time for that as the last of the Queen Wound's light, purple as a bruise, is extinguished and the first cracks in the Depths begin to flood.

— 38 —

And just like that, the walls splinter, and we are all pebbles in the current. The waters surge into the Gravemind's chamber as the Queen Wound continues to implode with each freed soul spinning out into the air, a whole flock of them like a school of fish that disappear as soon as you look at them. The waters rise around our knees, waists, and arms. I hold tight to Moss the same way Gourd clings to Dad.

"We need to reach higher ground," I splutter, fighting to float and keep seawater out of my mouth.

The salt sting of the ocean surges in my eyes and makes me squint as the waters continue to carry us up, up, up to the opening we entered through at the bottom of the great gray stone bowl. My mind spins as I shake one of the previously captive Reapers, a Shard Reaper with bleached white cornrows, urging her to wake up. We must swim for our lives.

We are near the top of the bowl now, but strong currents threaten to suck us back down. A small whirlpool spins Dirge over near me. The fourteen-year-old super-soldier's head bobs up and down, hands splayed, trying to catch the edge of the bowl where Moss and I are clinging to its side as if it is the last thing we will ever do.

And it might be.

I snag Dirge's arm and feel the snarling current nearly yank my arm from its socket. A yell escapes me but is lost in the chaos. I see Gourd, shielding Zay and Dad, her free arm pointing up toward the central spire. I grit my teeth, put aside the pain in my shoulder, and focus on dragging Dirge through the water and back to me.

"Thanks, Cap, I thought I was a goner." Dirge huffs, trying to blow saltwater from up her nose.

"Don't mention it. But we've got only a few seconds before this bowl overflows and we're doomed."

"Damn, this really wasn't how I wanted to go," Dirge replies.

My mind spins as fast as the current as more stone begins to crack with the pressure of the shattering curse and the ocean lurking beyond. "Can I interest you in a plan that involves breaking things?"

I don't have to ask her twice. I barely have to ask once, honestly.

Pointing to the rope bridge, the wet slap of thousands of gallons of seawater breaking through eats my orders, but Dirge understands instantly. She braces herself against me so she can focus the shot of her crossbow on the rope bridge above us. The Stormbolt yips, then whistles as it flies toward one end of the bridge and explodes with a clap of thunder. The bridge falls through the air toward us—and thankfully most of the structure is still intact and attached at the other end.

The rope bridge comes clattering down, and I help first Moss then Dirge up onto it before climbing up it myself. Summoning my winds, I swing the ladder close enough to Gourd, Zay, Dad, and the other Reaper captives. They scramble up the rope ladder after me.

Fountains of water burst from the walls as I climb with energy I didn't realize I had, and we are going up, up, up. My lungs are on fire as chunks of rock and debris collapse below, pummeling the gray stone bowl to dust and memory.

We are up the spire now, gunning hard and fast toward the *Chainbreaker*. Zay and Dirge pull level with me as a nearly unconscious Moss is draped over my shoulder like a sack of rice.

"Tell the Reapers that there's a narrow pa—"

But they don't need to be told. They can see another bridge, the one that leads directly to our ship—with forty Pointers standing in our way, bracing for a fight. The stone ceiling of the cave is already webbed with widening cracks, so there's no time to strategize. I hand Moss off behind me to a kindly man with the elaborate eye tattoos of a Reaper of Palm. I summon both wind-blades to my Reaper gauntlets, and we fall upon the Children of the Shark. The Pointer I'm facing dodges a blade and hisses before jabbing me directly in my chest, nearly knocking the wind from my lungs before I sweep its leg and swing the wind-blade down hard into the shark-demon's chest.

"COME ON!" I beckon, pointing to the bridge as more boulders begin to collapse down and into the river beyond.

We must make it across this bridge. I grunt, running harder as my crew, my dad, Sunshower, and the rest of the captured Reapers shove off from their battles with the Children of the Shark and are hot on my heels across the bridge. I stand at the end, counting as one, then five, then eight, and finally all thirteen of us are across with the hissing Pointers in vicious pursuit, muscles tensed and fangs bared.

I turn to Dirge with a devilish smile that she returns.

"Another plan that involves breaking things?" Dirge asks hopefully, casually picking off a Pointer that falls squealing into the river below.

"Together this time, but yes," I answer, conjuring my own storm around my hands.

"Y'know"—Dirge's storm-fist mirrors mine—"eventually, you're going to have to get your own signature moves."

"Yo, are y'all gonna punch this bridge or not?!" Zay says insistently as the Pointers are nearly across and many more are scaling the far wall to traverse the distance to us.

Dirge and I smile at each other, then at the Pointers, who haven't yet realized that they're trapped. The hunger behind their eyes does not waver as our fists slam down and the bridge crumbles, trapping the Children of the Shark behind us as the only way back turns to dust.

But there's no time to celebrate as the water above us sprays out from the walls. And just like that, we are all running again without a word. We are hustling over rocks, dodging stalactites, and everyone is grunting some form of *Keep going, keep going. We are almost—*

There.

Scroll and the other Windthreader, Ayo, are already prepared for us, likely ready since the moment they heard the cracking of the cave. I feel the power of the *Chainbreaker* flood my veins as the bubble of wind closes over the ship just in time for the waters to break through entirely and toss the ship out into the ocean. Shock waves nearly knock me over, but I flex my legs and urge the *Chainbreaker* toward the surface as the Depths implode behind us.

I push my mind to the calm space of the windbubble, wrestling my heartbeat until it slows.

And I feel the ship thrum to life beneath me as I think *air* and *up* and *home* and *free* and *not here.* As the surface looms ahead, I realize that these have always been words that meant the same thing.

— 39 —

More noise than I know what to do with greets the *Chainbreaker* as we erupt from the water to a sky purple as my name. The windbubble bursts, and the seawater showers us like rain. I hear raucous chants and calls from the circling Reaper ships. The decks of the *Stormblade, Glasstide, Sagewind,* and *Wavetamer* are lined with cheering Reapers.

I look over at Dad, half his locks shocked white, and he's draped over Gourd's arm for balance. I can see my reflection in his eyes as he lowers himself to one knee and at long last throws his arms around me.

"Violet Moon, you are some kind of miracle," he rumbles into my neck, his voice finally real to me again.

"Violet *Chainbreaker*," Gourd corrects Dad, the largest smile on her face I've ever seen.

"I couldn't be prouder, Violet Chainbreaker." He pauses, jaw trembling.

Violet Moon, Violet Chainbreaker, Violet the Reaper, Violet the Daughter of the Five Heavens—all my many names I didn't know I had. I allow a laugh to ripple through my chest, the euphoria of seeing the sky again filling me with enough emotion for five Violets. I've never been so many people, and truly the stars have never shone brighter.

I feel my knees almost buckle as the sky rings with chants.

CHAINBREAKER.

CHAINBREAKER.

CHAINBREAKER.

I pull Dad in tighter. I can smell the coconut and sea-salt smell of his beard, and I can feel the rough calluses of his hands cupping my face as he vibrates with emotion.

I take a deep breath as Dad gets helped to his feet by Gourd. A fierce grin washes over his face as I look out over the tides, scanning ahead for the *Moony*. And the *Moony* is on the tides but not where I'm looking. Not out and ahead over the waters where our ancestors fought and lived and sang and built and were stolen and reclaimed. Not over the lilac and teal of the sea I pushed my father's funeral boat out into. No, it isn't in any of those places. Instead, the *Moony* is where it's been all twelve years of my life—right at our side.

Already the crew is hammering the sides of the ship in celebration as the *Moony* lowers a rope ladder onto our deck. The song and celebration swell above our heads as Mooneye practically spills over the side and into the arms of his brother. Sunshower and Mooneye have never looked more identical than they do now, heads thrown back in laughter and disbelief. And it isn't long before the other ships follow suit, tossing down ropes and retrieving everyone they thought they might never see again.

Moss sidles up beside me, and I lift him off the ground, spinning in place—and nearly trip over my boots on the slick surface. Thankfully nobody sees, but even if they did, I don't think anyone would remember that little detail when Moss's grin is so wide it shames the moon. Zay, Zay's mom, and Dirge gossip in the corner as Zay, all business, seems to be walking his mom through how the crossbow he built for Dirge works. I guess some people's work is never *really* done.

And with the light dimming over our heads, I could swear I've never seen so many stars. Maybe each is an ancestor we helped free; maybe the light is the last story they never stop telling us.

A disbelieving laugh rolls through my body as I think of how Reaping will be different with six ships instead of five, but that can wait till tomorrow, or next week. Or whenever I wake up, because the weariness in my bones is something not even the ancestors have a name for.

Or maybe we are the last of the Reapers, with the Depths undone and collapsed.

Maybe one day there will be no ships and no chains, no fevers, and no word for *master*. There will be no need for Reapers, and no one will fall from a ship that kept them captive.

For now, I stand on the deck of my ship with my friends,

and all our lost ones are no longer lost to us. As I gaze up, the last purple lights in the sky disappear, and even the constellations seem to applaud.

The skies don't weep for us, they welcome us, protect us, celebrate us in a hundred languages we can't name. But I know what they're saying:

You were not born for tragedy, just look at you; you've already built your Heaven right where you are.

CREDITS

Editors: Brian Geffen and Carina Licon
Agents: Patrice Caldwell and Trinica Sampson-Vera
Designer: Aurora Parlagreco
Production Editor: Kristen Stedman
Production Manager: Allene Cassagnol
Copyeditor: Mindy Fichter
Proofreaders: Ana Deboo and Courtney Jordan